Chi-Town Hood Affairs

Part 2

By Nicole Black

Dedication

Grandma,

You were....

The strongest woman I have ever met.

You were....

A woman that touched the lives of many.

You were....

A savior to those in need.

You are....

An angel now.

Mrs. Inez Jackson, I didn't hear you all those times you said, "get up of your narrow a** and do something with yourself." Now that you're gone, I find it crazy that I hear you loud and clear. I took that advice and it landed me in a position to write this message. Hopefully you're looking down on me with pride in your eyes. May you continue to rest in peace.

Acknowledgments

I thank God for giving me this talent that I didn't know existed within me until I hit a rough patch in life. God really works in mysterious ways.

Jinnie Jackson, I LOVE YOU!!! No words can describe how much I appreciate all you do for me. You are the definition of a STRONG WOMAN! I wouldn't trade you for the world. Thanks for being the best mother ever!

My little/big man Jamari, I can't imagine life without you. I love you to pieces son.

Tammy, Carolyn, Kris, Michael, Breard, Erick, Zack, Shun, Raymond, Lyric, Peanut, Moo-Moo, Aaron, and the rest of my family, all of you mean a lot to me. I love y'all!!

Shamarco, Shunta, Mallory, Dee, Eric, J-baby, Brandon Tiff, Dominique, Shun, Shevitta, Mike, Larry, Cardell, Linda, and Meechi, thanks for all of the support you give me and for always being there for me. All of y'all are stuck with me for life. Special thanks to Meechi for lending me your name for the series.

I would like to give a very special thank you to the best publisher ever! It can't get no better than Myss Shan! Thank you for being the wonderful, talented, inspirational woman that you are. To the talented ladies of Shan Presents and the men and women of The Bankroll Squad, I wish each and every one of you much success as you go on this journey.

Shoutout to Lefty, Donte, Rio, Anthony, Khadija, Dorothy, Carmen, Barbara, LaToya, Guam, and everyone else that, bought, read, borrowed, supported, and promoted this book. From the bottom of my heart I appreciate it.

Text SHAN to 22828 to stay up to date with new releases, sneak peeks, and more.

Blam, Blam, Blam, Blam.

Boom, Boom, Boom, Boom.

Blam, Blam, Blam.

Boom, Boom, Boom, Boom, Boom.

Somethin' pierced my flesh before I fell to the ground. Zell put one in my leg making me instantly fall. I looked up towards the street to see Zell's Audi speeding away from the curb. Noticing Starks lying face down in the grass, I hopped up and limped over to him to make sure he was good.

He ran out of bullets and had to hit the ground. I looked over my shoulder and saw Anaya still lying on the ground. I already knew she was gone. She wasn't breathing, and she had a hole in the back of her head. Blood and brain matter was spilling into the grass. I'd seen a lot in the hood, but I couldn't stand to look at her like that.

"Damn she ain't deserve that." I shook my head.

"You need to go to the hospital," Starks said as he looked at my bloody leg.

"I'm cool."

Starks looked over at Anaya. "Damn. God bless the dead."

Cola and Kee came out of the house first. Both of them were screaming at the sight of Anaya dead on the ground. Everybody else ran out right behind them. When Cola saw my leg, she lost it. You would have thought I was dying the way Cola was crying and screaming. Londyn ran out of the house not knowing what was going on. I hid my leg from her and turned her away from Anaya until B came to get her.

Big Curt was the first to speak to me, "It was him?"

"Hell yeah."

"Who?" Cola asked wit' tears in her eyes. At that point, I had to tell her. I said fuck it and told everybody at the same time. Jazzy was helping my aunt and uncle keep the kids in line. She didn't hear me when I told my people her brother was responsible for this.

Jay and the rest of my niggas were ready to put in work. I knew my leg would slow me down. I wanted to be healed before anybody made a move on Zell. When the time came, I didn't want no setbacks. And if I wasn't there to pull the trigger, it was gon' be some problems.

Jazzy walked over to us after all of the kids were rounded up. All conversation stopped when she walked up. I'm guessing she thought by helping Kira fight Anaya; she would prove somethin' to us. She was wrong. It wasn't no way in hell somebody related to the nigga I was about to kill was about to be a part of my circle.

I ignored the pain I was starting to feel and told everybody, "When the police come, it was a drive-by. We ain't see shit. We don't know shit. We ain't telling shit." Everybody agreed.

"What's understood ain't gotta be explained. Call 911 Kira," Jake instructed. Without hesitation, she pulled out her phone and made the call.

Nurse Cookie helped Aunt Carla put some of the kids in the car. She wanted to get them away from the commotion. Londyn had a fit when B put her in the car. She knew somethin' was wrong. I told Cola to put on a happy face for Londyn's sake. After Cola talked to her, she calmed down a lot.

The police and ambulance arrived ten minutes later. They put a white sheet over Anaya and took me to St. Bernard Hospital. Cola rode in the ambulance wit' me while everybody else followed in their cars. The police looked at each other suspiciously when only one person stayed back with Anaya.

It was in Nurse Cookie's nature because of her line of work to stay wit' Anaya. None of us had ties to Anaya. We didn't have a reason to stay behind. I knew they would probably come question us since Anaya was beat up. We would get a story together about that a lil' later.

The bullet went in and out. The doctor wanted me to have crutches, but I wasn't feeling the idea of having four legs or taking antibiotics. I hated pills.

"Were you going to tell me he saw us?" Cola asked when everybody left the room. Cola didn't think it was possible for me to be touched. I always told her I was not invincible. Just because I'd been in the streets for over ten years and had never been shot didn't mean it couldn't happen. I was lucky all those years. Shit, I was lucky today. It could have easily been me under that white sheet.

"Yeah I was. After the party was over."

"I'm worried now. What if he saw Londyn or followed them to Miss Carla's house?"

"B know to keep his eyes open. If he followed them, trust me he would be dead as soon as he tried to run up in the house. Besides he already hit me and told me everything is good. He knows what car to look out for."

"I'm not staying in that house, Baker. I don't feel safe anymore."

"I wouldn't ask you to stay there. Co, I told you I would keep you safe and die for you if need be. I mean that shit from the bottom of my heart. It ain't a nigga alive that can touch you and live to talk about it. Straight up. You know what he was doing over there?"

"No. You think his sister had anything to do with him finding us?"

"Nah, baby I don't." That was the honest truth. I didn't think Jazzy fucked wit' Zell, but she struck me as the type of chick that would do anything for a buck.

It was a mystery how Zell knew where we were. The only people that knew where we were staying were the ones out in the waiting room. I knew my people wasn't wit' the disloyal shit. If they were, shit was gon' get bloody. One thing I hated was a disloyal muthafucka around me.

When I got released from the hospital the next morning, everybody was still here. Me and Cola got in the car wit' Big Curt and Kimmy. They had a house out in Lansing that looked like a mini mansion. It was more than enough room for everybody to stay there. Starks opted not to stay. He wanted to be in his own space, which was understandable after being locked up for four years.

Any block or building I had dope on or in got shut down until further notice. None of us was hurting for money. That move wouldn't put a dent in our pockets. Besides Big Curt was my connect, and he knew what was going on. Our business relationship wouldn't be damaged behind this situation.

The next two weeks went by fast. My leg was as good as new. Before I could get Zell, I had to make sure my lil lady was in another state. Aunt Carla and B were taking her to Disneyland, and then they were going to see my aunt that lived in

Bakersfield, California for three weeks. A month was more than enough time to get rid of Zell's bitch ass.

Zell

I couldn't believe I saw that bitch Cola hugged up wit' that nigga Baker. That explained the license plate on that Range she was drivin' that day. Snake ass bitch. At first, I felt bad about violatin' her the way I did, now I didn't. As much as I loved her, she turned out to be just like every other woman in my life. That was why I did these bitches the way I did.

My mind wouldn't let what I saw go. She'd been playin' me the whole time. I wanted to put a bullet in both of them. When that front door opened, I got ready. I saw Anaya and Starks walk out, then Baker. All of them was probably in on this together. I had my pistol on my lap waitin' to make my move.

I saw Baker walkin' further out the house. That was when I hit the corner and let off in their direction. I heard through the grapevine about Anaya. Oh well, bitch shouldn't have been in the way. I knew I hit Baker when I saw him fall.

Nobody had seen or heard from Starks since that day.

Takin' a sip of the Ciroc, I watched Kee's house like a hawk waitin' for one of them to come home. Somebody was bound to come back to the house. When they did, I was gon' be right here waitin'.

For the past couple weeks, I'd been sittin' here watchin' and waitin'. Only time I left was to eat and take a shower at my new crib. I would have been a fool to stay in the crib I took Cola to. That would be the first place they would go to find me.

It was dark outside when I saw a beat up old Bonneville pull up in front of the house. I counted three bodies inside the car. Both passengers got out of the car wit' their hats low over their eyes. They both looked around cautiously. When they reached the door, one pried it open wit' a crowbar while the other looked out.

The driver got out and popped the trunk of the car. The two passengers were still inside the house. They came out minutes later wit' about six duffle bags. They each had three bags apiece. They went back in and came out carrying a fifty-inch TV. The one that got out of the back went back to close the door. Either they planned on goin' back and gettin' more stuff or they just wanted everything to appear normal. Oddly, he didn't get back in the car. The car pulled off as he walked in my direction.

"Aye."

He turned towards me wit' a scowl on his face. "Fuck is you?"

"A friend of Baker's. I heard he got shot. I'm tryin' to check up on my homie. I can't get in touch wit' him."

He lit a cigarette and adjusted his hat even lower than what it was. "Yo' homie died at the hospital yesterday mornin'."

Although it caught me by surprise, hearin' that was music to my ears. I was happy that nigga was dead. He took my bitch from me, and he had never been a broke nigga. Baker needed to be six feet under. Now I could run the streets. I was gonna be on top in no time. I needed to know about Starks, too.

"What about Starks?"

"Muthafucka you askin' too many fuckin' questions."

"I don't mean no harm. These my people."

"Starks good. Now I suggest you leave before you end up like Baker." He raised his shirt to expose his pistol. "Come 'round here again, watch what happens to you."

Normally, I would have let this nigga feel some heat. But I got what I needed, and I liked his heart. I had unfinished business wit' Starks. It was time to pay my holier than thou mother a visit to get Miss Carla's address.

I drove west down 63rd street until I got to 63rd and Artesian. All of Vee's lights were off. That was perfect for me. It didn't take much to get in. The door on her house was cheap as hell. One hard shoulder bump against it, I was in.

I walked through the house checkin' the rooms; nobody was home. I turned her livin' room light on, sat in her husband's leather chair, and kicked my feet up on the coffee table.

"Shoot, I must have left that light on all day. That dang light bill is going to be sky high," I heard her say a little while later. She walked in surprised to see me sittin' there.

"How you doin' mama? Nice to see that hot water didn't do too much damage to yo' face." Behind her was a man that wasn't her husband. I knew that from lookin' at the weddin' picture on the wall. "I see you still out here bein' a hoe. Do yo' pastor husband know you still good for nothin' but spreadin' yo' legs?"

"I'm about to call the police."

"That will be the last call you ever make," I said as she stood there lookin' at the man she was wit'. "My man if you like yo' life, leave right now." The man bolted out the door faster than a track star.

"What do you want Dezell? I don't socialize with criminals."

"Bitch save it. You out here still sellin' yo' old ass pussy, and you turnin' yo' nose up at me. Fuck outta here. And don't call me by my real name."

"I pray for you and your sister every night. Lord knows..." she looked at the ceiling as if she could see God, "...I made mistakes, but I gave him my life."

"Yeah, yeah, yeah. I need Carla Wallace's address."

"Why?"

"Bitch because I do."

"Stop disrespecting me. I'm your mother."

"What type of mother sucks her own son's dick? What type of mother disowns her own daughter? What kind of mother sells her pussy and gets high? Mother my ass. You ain't shit but a waste of a soul." Thinkin' about that shit took me back. I may would have been normal if she wouldn't have done that shit to me.

"Every saint has a past and every sinner has a future. I made mistakes, and I'm sorry, Dezell."

"Sorry ain't gon' make me normal again." She wasn't sorry. She didn't wanna die tonight; that was all. Bitch turned me into a woman hater and now she was sorry. "Give me the address." She shook her head no.

One was already in the chamber for a situation like this. Standin' up, I walked closer to her. I towered over her; she had fear all over her face. Vee didn't know I had a gun until I shot her in the arm.

Pop.

She let out a loud cry for help. I warned her to shut up by putting the gun to her head. "Give me the fuckin' address." Once again she shook her head no.

Pop.

"Ooooh, Jesus," she screamed. This time her leg had a hole in it.

"Dezell, why are you--."

"What I tell you about that Dezell shit?"

"What do you want with Carla? What has she done to you?" she asked between grunts.

"Nothin'." It was true. I honestly didn't want Carla. I wanted her son. If she didn't give him up she would be wit' her dead nephew.

"Lord have mercy," she grimaced in pain. "What do you want to know where she lives for then?"

"Look you don't need to know all that. Are you gon' give me the address or not?"

"I would rather die before I—"

Pop, Pop, Pop.

She said she would rather die, so I gave her what she wanted. I searched the whole house lookin' for an address book. She always kept one when I was younger for her tricks. I found what I was lookin' for upstairs in Vee's bedroom tucked in a shoebox. I ripped out the page that had Carla's address on it and put it in my pocket.

I made my way downstairs to leave when I heard the front door close. It was her husband. He had two suitcases wit' him. He called out to Vee.

"Honey, I caught an earlier flight." Honey? He was a lame ass nigga. I tucked my pistol in my waist before headin' towards the door.

Walkin' past him, I patted him on that back. "What's up step-dad?"

The state of confusion he was in brought a smile to my face. I'm sure Vee never mentioned Jazzy or me to him. This shouldn't have been the way we met, but shit happened.

On my way back East on 63rd street, my phone rang. It was a number I didn't recognize; I hit ignore. It rang again, and again, and again. I still ignored it. I didn't answer for numbers I didn't recognize. I kept driving until I swerved at the sound of gunshots comin' from behind me.

Boom. Boom.

Boom. Boom. Boom.

A silver Camaro was right behind me. The passenger had the window rolled down just enough for me to see the muzzle of the gun sticking out. I swerved around a car that was stopped at a red light. I made a right on Western Street. To my surprise the car wasn't behind me. I had shit I needed to do. Wasn't no mufucka takin' me out tonight.

My car didn't have a single hole in it. I was lucky they missed. Whoever this was didn't have no aim. I raced down the street wit' no destination until my phone rang again. It was another number that I didn't know.

"What?" I answered.

A man's voice spoke, "What up doe?"

"Who the fuck is this?" I asked wit' a frown on my face. I didn't know who this nigga was or why he was calling me.

"Damn you forgot about me already? When you shot at me, you should have killed me nigga."

"Baker?" I asked surprised.

"The one and only. Hold on I got somebody that wanna holla at you."

"Ex bro in law what the fuck is up?" a different voice said.

"Jay?"

"Bitch ass nigga," Jay said before Baker's voice came back through the phone.

"Next time you shoot at me make sure you kill me. Be careful. You never know when death will come knocking at the door."

"Fuck nigga," I heard Jay yell in the background before the phone hung up.

Jay and Baker still alive; damn. I had to stay on my toes for real now. Cola was a good ass actress. Them fake tears she cried had me thinkin' that nigga was really dead. She knew what I did the whole time. Who was that nigga that told me Baker was dead?

This all explained why Feek and Spook was missin' in action. I got played more than once. If these niggas were gon' try to take me out I was gonna be ready for their ass.

Boom.

Boom.

Boom.

"Ah shit!" I yelled out in pain.

Cola

A few days ago, I found out I was having twins; two boys at that. Baker was elated about having two sons. He was so happy they would be born at the same time he couldn't stop smiling. I was excited about my baby boys, as well. I hope Londyn adjusted to having two little brothers. I rubbed my stomach and smiled at the thought of having two more kids with the love of my life.

I was starting to worry about Baker because he'd been gone for hours. He was out in Crown Point Indiana with Big Curt and the rest of the guys meeting with their gun supplier. Ever since Zell shot him, I hadn't wanted Baker to leave my side. I was scared Zell had been following us or something. I didn't know how his crazy ass found us in the first damn place.

"It's about time. Baker, you been gone for hours," I said to him when he walked in with food. I wanted to jump up and hug him, but I knew he was tired of me doing that when he came home.

"I had to take care of somethin'. I got you somethin' to eat," Baker said as he passed me the two slices of pizza for Papa John's.

"Mmmm." My eyes rolled in the back of my head after I took a bite out of the pizza. It was like an orgasm in my mouth. It was that good. I forgot what I said to Baker after that bite of pizza.

Baker looked at me like I was crazy. "Damn Co. Yo' ass ain't eating pizza again." Baker looked at the pizza like he hated it, and I burst out laughing.

"Awww my baby jealous," I said as I got up to hug him. He played like he wasn't gon' hug me back at first then he wrapped his arms around me. I always got that safe feeling when Baker hugged me. Even though things still happened to me, I knew he would protect me at all costs if he can.

"Hell yeah. You lucky I ain't put one in that pizza," he chuckled. His face turned serious. "Zell, know me and Jay alive now."

I leaned back. "How he know that?"

"I told him after that fake break in at Kee's crib. He asked Jake mans, Roc that ran in the crib about me. Roc hit me when he saw him. I told him to tell Zell I died at the hospital. Since we were all the way in Crown Point, I told Roc what to do. That's why I called and asked you for his number. I called him and let him hear me and Jay voice. Don't leave this house for nothing until I tell you to Co."

"Okay. Baker, I feel bad about Anaya. I didn't like her for what she did at my barbecue, but she should still be alive."

"Life is funny like that. He killed her because she was in the wrong place at the wrong time. I feel bad about it, too, baby. I couldn't even look at her laying on the ground like that."

"I wish I wouldn't have fought her." I really did regret that fight. Even if Anaya had lived, I would regret fighting her. I was about to be a wife; I have a daughter, and I'm pregnant. All of those things told me I was too old to be fighting.

Baker took one hand from around me and rubbed my stomach. "I wish you wouldn't have either. I'm still pissed off at yo' ass for putting my lil ones at risk."

"I'm sorry."

"You better be. Aye, I'm about to go set some shit up. You gon' be good here for a minute?" Baker asked in between planting kisses on my neck. He was getting me hot and bothered. I start unbuckling his Gucci belt, and he pulled away from me.

"Why you pull away?"

"That's for making me jealous wit' that pizza," he laughed.

"I hate you so much," I laughed, too.

Baker gave me a long, passionate kiss. "I'll be back in a couple hours baby."

An hour after Baker left, the doorbell rang. Big Curt had a security system that saw every square inch of the inside and outside of his house. I turned the TV to channel three. I looked at the small square section that showed the front door. I maximized it to full screen. The person on the other side of that door sent chills down my spine.

I stared at the screen as he continued to knock on the door. This was the last person I wanted to see. I watched as he called someone on his phone. Seconds later, he was walking inside the house. I had been purposely staying out of his way, now I was about to be alone with him.

"You was just gon' leave me out there?" his voice startled me. I was lost in my own thoughts. "What if somebody was after me?" He searched my face waiting for a response. "You cool?"

"I'm good." When I tried to brush past him, he grabbed my arm. "Can you let go of me? How you get in here?"

Starks let me go and backed away from me. "You know Big Curt got some high tech stuff. He unlocked the door from his phone." Big Curt could have worked on computers. He loved technology almost as much as he loved selling weight. "Stop acting funny towards me, Serenity. I told you I wouldn't tell Baker about what happened."

"Put yourself in my shoes. Before you went to jail, we were talking about being together. It's hard for me to keep this secret that I know will make Baker look at me differently."

"I feel you. What happened in the past is gon' stay there. Baker won't know unless you tell him. I can't be around him sometimes behind our past. That's why I didn't stay here." Starks looked sincere when he spoke. I was in a bind, and I didn't know what to do.

"Try sleeping next to him every night and waking up to him holding you every morning."

"I ain't trying to do all that," Starks joked to lighten the mood. "I got one question for you."

"What's that?"

"All those times I wrote you, why you ain't write me back?"

"Ummmm you never wrote me."

"Yes I did. I sent some letters to Kee's crib. I sent a letter every couple months the first year I was locked up. When you ain't drop me no lines, I gave up."

"I never got them, Starks. What did they say?" I never received letters from Starks. Kee checked the mail at the house in the city twice a week when she got off work. Not once did she bring me a letter from him. Starks had to be lying.

"That's not important now. Instead of me still thinking you had the out of sight out of mind mentality about me, now I know why you didn't write back." He was right it didn't matter what the letters said now. I was with Baker, and he was all that mattered.

"Leaving you in there wondering about me is something I would have never done. If I would have gotten the letters, I would have written you back. Around that time, I was going through a lot. I would have vented my frustrations out through a letter."

"One more question, Serenity. Was that my baby all those years ago?"

"Starks we talked about this plenty of times. It was not your baby." There was no way I would tell him the truth about that. Sometimes men liked to use things against you. If he ever decided to tell Baker about our past relationship, I could probably talk him into staying with me if he wanted to leave. Me possibly carrying his cousin's child would definitely leave me without Baker and without this ring on my finger.

"Aight. Well, if you need me, I'll be around here somewhere."

"Okay."

I heard footsteps coming up the stairs. I hoped and prayed whoever was coming up the steps didn't hear anything that Starks and I said to each other. I looked to my left and saw my brother with a look of disappointment on his face. He motioned with his head for me to follow him to his bedroom.

Once there, I sat in a chair next to his bed while he locked the bedroom door. I was trying to read Jay, but got nothing. I knew he was about to be the little big brother and get on me.

"Sis, you know I fucks wit' you the long way right?"

Here it comes. I know he heard Starks and I talking. "Jay, I know it's a shock to you. But it's not like that."

"What's it like then sis? We under the same roof and I ain't spent no time wit' you in weeks. Why you been neglecting me?"

Relieved he didn't hear anything, I became less tense. "Awww, I'm sorry, Jay. Let me find out you in touch with your sensitive side."

"Girl stop. I just I miss spending time wit' you."

"I miss that too big head." It clicked to me why Jay was acting like this. Our mother's birthday approaching was the trigger of Jay's emotions.

"I been thinking about mama. Sometimes I wish I was wit' her. That lady was the shit. I miss her so much sis." Jay always had sad eyes when he mentioned our mother.

"Jay, you about to make me cry. When it's time for you to be with mama, you will be. Don't let me hear you say you wish that again. What would I do without you? What about Londyn, Baker, Kee, and your nephews that will be born in a few months? Not to mention Jake and everybody else that loves you. I miss her, too, but I know mama is with us in our hearts, Jay. She's always watching over us." Jay just had me all emotional talking about our mother and him saying he wished he was with her. My life wouldn't feel right if Jay wasn't in it.

"If I could just have a conversation wit' her."

"You can have that any time you want, Jay. She might not say anything back, but she hears you."

Jay and I sat around and reminisced about our mother for hours. We had stories for days about her. Somewhere in between stories our father called to check on us. He was in the same joint as Jay's street mentor, Meechi and his childhood friend Richie.

Richie was serving life for killing the person that killed him and Jay's best friend Sean. Jay was lucky Richie lived by the code of no snitching. If he didn't, Jay would be exactly where Richie was. We got a chance to talk to them both after our father talked to us.

Richie and Jay together was always nonstop laughs. I had tears in my eyes from laughing so hard. Meechi still had a thing for me after all these years. He was gon' have to keep having it because Baker was all I wanted.

I was tired and could no longer keep my eyes open. I fell asleep in Jay's bed not long after we hung up with Meechi. I woke up in the middle of the night to go to the bedroom Baker, and I was sleeping in. When I reached the room, the door was slightly open. I saw Baker lying in bed in nothing but his boxers flipping through the channels. Just as I was about to push the door open, I heard Kee's voice.

"We need to tell Cola about us. You think she'll be mad, Baker?"

"Probably will. We been keeping it from her for a minute," Baker responded.

"I feel so bad," Kee said.

"Yo' ass should feel bad," Baker laughed.

Jay interjected, "Both of y'all muthafuckas should feel bad about this shit."

"Bruh you just as guilty as the both of us," Baker said through laughter.

Their voices made me so mad that I didn't know what to do with myself. I just walked away from the door. If I had stayed, it would be some dying, crying, and flower buying for all three of them no good muthafuckas.

My ears had to have been deceiving me. Baker and Kee have been fuckin' behind my back. My own brother knew about the betrayal and deceit from the two people that were supposed to love me oh so much. I was so pissed and hurt that I left the house without saying anything to anybody.

I walked around this unfamiliar neighborhood with no destination in mind. I could see headlights approaching me. I didn't care to turn around. It could have been Zell, but I was so far gone, I didn't give a damn who it was. My vision was blurred from the tears in my eyes. I tried hard not to let them fall. They had a mind of their own and rolled down my face.

A big pit-bull barked at me from behind the gate of a house as I walked by. I gave the dog the finger as if it knew what that meant. I felt my heart break into a million pieces over and over again. The thought of Baker and Kee being intimate had me on the verge of a panic attack. Baker was my heart. How could he do this to me? I was consumed with so much sadness I hadn't noticed the car pull up on the side of me.

"It's too late for you to be out here walking. Let me take you home."

"Go away," I said without looking at the car.

"What kind of man would I be if I let you stay out here walking at 2:30 in the morning?"

"One that would honor what I want and leave me the fuck alone." The car pulled off fast, only to get ahead of me. The driver got out of the car and walked back towards me.

"What happened? Why you out here?" I ignored him. "Guess we gon' be on a silent walk. I'm not leaving you out here. You might as well tell me what's wrong." Still, I didn't say anything to him until I heard him say, "Aye Baker, I'm out here and yo'---."

I slapped Starks' phone out of his hand; it shattered on the concrete. "Who asked you to call him?"

"You ain't have to break my phone. I know he don't know you out here. That's why I called him."

"Why are you out here this late?"

"I went to get somethin'. Now what's wrong?"

"Nothing, I can't go back to that house right now. If I do, your cousin will end up dead," I snapped.

"It's a hotel up the street. I'll get you a room for the rest of the night. That's cool?"

"Better than sleeping next to a liar."

***

Starks walked me up to my room to make sure I got there safe. I sat on the bed and thought about Baker and Kee. The image of them having sex was as clear as day in my mind. I could see Baker making the same faces he made when we had sex. Kee kissing and touching all over his body pissed me off even more. The part that killed me the most was Jay. I don't even have words to describe how I felt about Jay right now. I did know I wanted to whoop ass. Kee's ass, Baker's ass, and Jay's ass. In that muthafuckin' order.

"You a'ight, Serenity?" Starks' voice broke my train of thought. "Baker probably going crazy thinking somethin' happened to you."

"Was he crazy about me when he was fuckin' my best friend? Huh? Was his ass worried then? I bet he wasn't!" I yelled. Starks was getting on my last nerve steady talking about Baker this and Baker that. Fuck Baker! And fuck Starks for steady talking about him.

"Baker love you to death. He wouldn't do nothing like that to you," Starks said with sincerity in his eyes.

"If I wouldn't have heard it with my own ears I would believe you."

"You must have thought you heard that. Baker ain't that type of man."

"I know what I heard." My mind drifted back to what I heard hours ago. I was hurt beyond repair. Kee of all people; my best friend. I wondered how her job would feel if they knew she indulged in weed on a regular basis. Baker was the love of my life, and he betrayed me. My own brother knew about it. I let the tears cascade down my face without trying to stop them.

"I still think you wrong. If I had a phone, I would call him to clear this up. Before I knew who you were, I could tell how much he loved you by the way he talked about you. I know my cousin, and he wouldn't do that."

"Yeah okay." My emotions got the best of me, and I asked Starks something that had been on my mind ever since he told me he used to write me. "You ever wonder what it would be like if I got your letters?"

Starks looked me deep in my eyes. "I used to before I found out you were my cousin's girl. I used to wonder what it would be like to wake up next to you, go out wit' you, spoil you, and other things. I ain't gon' lie I was in the joint sick wondering why you ain't write me back. I always thought about you, Serenity."

"I wondered things, too."

"All that don't matter now."

I leaned over to lay my head on his shoulder. He didn't move or say a word. He looked like he was in deep thought. I kissed him on his cheek. When he didn't protest, I turned his head to face me. We shared a long passionate kiss. He placed both of his hands on my face while he stuck his tongue in my mouth. I almost melted from his touch. We rolled around on the bed kissing and touching each other like we used to way back when.

Starks bit my neck gently as I lightly scratched his back. His strong hands gripped my ass firmly while he continued to nibble on my neck. Starks picked me up, and I wrapped my legs around his waist. Our tongues explored each other's mouths again like we were searching for a hidden treasure.

We began to undress each other at the same time. Starks kicked his shoes off while I unzipped his pants. He pulled his shirt over his head to reveal his bare chest. I waited in anticipation for him to undress me. Starks pulled my peach colored maxi dress over my head, and then he froze in place.

"What's the matter?"

Starks closed his eyes and shook his head. He took a deep breath. "This ain't right. I will always feel somethin' for you, but this can't go down. You pregnant by my cousin; it ain't right."

Starks turned his back to me after he gave me my dress to put back on. He put his clothes back on as well. I stared at my small round belly and silently thanked my unborn sons. Had I not been pregnant, Starks and I would have taken things too far. My hurt feelings had me thinking foolishly. Baker always said I was irrational when I was hurt. This proved he was right.

I was so embarrassed. I sat on the bed with my head down. Looking at Starks wasn't an option. I couldn't believe what I just tried to do.

"Thanks for stopping things before they got out of hand."

"It's nothing. I know you are acting off emotions. One of us had to be the bigger person."

"What if I wasn't acting off emotions?"

"What if cats could talk and pigs could fly? We will never know, Serenity. I'll sleep in this chair. I'm not leaving you by yourself."

"You don't have to stay," I said finally looking up at him.

"I'm staying."

Sleep didn't come easy for me that night. My thoughts were all over the place. I wondered if Baker and Kee were taking advantage of the fact that I wasn't in the house. They were probably sleeping like babies, while I was wide awake thinking about what they're doing. I thought Baker was the best man in the world, and he broke my heart.

What just happened with Starks was also on my mind. Baker was wrong for messing around with Kee; there was no doubt about that. However, I didn't have to take it there with Starks because of my broken heart. Maybe when I woke up this would just be a dream. My heart won't heal after this. I'd never be the same.

Baker

I took a hard hit off my blunt and blew smoke out of my mouth. I was still hot about a phone call I got not too long ago. Shit just fucked me all the way up. Smoking was my only hope to calm down.

Jake called me and told me Roc couldn't kill Zell because somebody called the police after Roc let off on Zell the first time. Instead of Roc doing the job right, he wanted play duck duck goose wit' the nigga. After I called Zell, Roc was supposed to kill him. He wasn't supposed to do shit before that. This was exactly why I liked doing shit myself. Niggas always had do some other shit. The only reason we used Roc was because all of us were damn near an hour away out in Crown Point. I knew Zell would be long gone by the time we made it to the city.

I was sitting at the table smoking my blunt in peace. Each time I hit the blunt; I cared less and less about Roc fuckin' up. When Kee walked in the kitchen wit' a worried look on her face, I already knew this high was about to be blown. She sat across from me at the table and looked at me like she couldn't find the words to say what she had to say. She mumbled somethin' to me, and I told her to spit that shit out. Ain't no need to beat around the bush about nothing.

"Fuck you mean she ain't in there? Where else she gon' be?" I barked at Kee after she told me Cola wasn't in Jay's room. I checked on her right after Jay and Kee came to my room to smoke before we all turned in. I had knocked out before I got a chance to go get Cola and bring her to our room.

"I don't know, Baker. I went to see if she was hungry. When I opened the door, the room was empty. I just searched everywhere for her. She is nowhere to be found," Kee said.

"Fuck y'all doing all this yelling for? People trying to sleep," Jay said when he walked in the kitchen yawning.

"Where Cola at, Jay?" I asked.

"In my room. You know that already."

"No, she not. She didn't tell you she was leaving?" I pulled out my phone to call her. That was no use. I could hear her phone ringing in Jay's room, which was right next to the kitchen.

"She didn't tell me shit. How long she been gone?"

"Nobody knows," Kee said.

"Look around the house again, Kee. I told her not to leave out. If that nigga Zell see her out somewhere he gon' do more than violate her." I clenched my teeth out of anger. Cola don't think shit through before she did shit sometimes. She knew it wasn't safe for her out here. It was too early for this fuck shit.

"Big Curt got cameras all over the place. Tell him to pull that shit up," Jay demanded. "And what you mean if Zell see her? Didn't Jake people handle that?"

I shook my head. "Hell nah. He managed to fuck that up."

Big Curt was coming out of the washroom when me and Jay approached him. We told him Cola was gone and nobody knew where she went. He pulled up the system on his living room TV. He fast-forwarded to the time when Jay left Cola in his room sleep. Big Curt fast-forwarded some more until I saw Cola come out of the room.

I pointed at the TV screen when I saw Cola appear in the hallway. I wanted to tell him to stop at a different point, but now wasn't the time for that. My focus right now was to make sure Cola was safe.

We watched as she made her way to the other side of the house to the bedroom we were in. She had her hand on the door like she was about to open it; all of a sudden she dropped her head and just stood there. I knew then she heard the conversation about Jay and Kee.

The camera showed her leaving the house. Big Curt pulled up the outside camera video. It showed Cola walking down the driveway wiping her face. I watched her until the video no longer showed her. I was pissed she left the house, but I hoped nothing foul happened to Co man. My heart wouldn't be able to take that.

"She heard us last night," I said when we were done watching the video.

Jay threw his hands in the air. "That shit got her that mad that she just left the house?"

"Obviously, it did. We need to go find her. I'm not sitting here while she out there pregnant wit' Zell's savage ass still alive," I said to Jay.

Jay sped through the streets like a racecar driver. We drove around for hours looking for Cola. I tried to call Starks a few times; his phone was going straight to voicemail. I left him three messages to call me back. I wanted him to look around the city. He never came back last night, so I figured he was already in the city.

Starks didn't answer or call back none while we were out. That was strange to me. One thing I could say about my cousin was he always answered his phone. If he didn't he would get back to me in minutes.

Jay broke my thoughts when he spoke, "Where could she be out here? Only people she know out here in Lansing is the ones that's out here looking for her. Let's go to the city and see if she out there. Big Curt can handle it out here."

"That ain't the question bruh. The question is why did she leave? Cola know what's up and she decide to leave in the middle of the night like ain't shit going on out here. I love yo' sister, but she do some dumb shit sometimes. Straight up."

"I already know." Jay shook his head and in a low tone he said, "I can't believe the shit I heard last night."

"What you say bruh?"

"Oh, I ain't say shit. Just thinking out loud."

"Aight, let's got to the city."

We rode around the streets of Chicago until it was dark outside. Big Curt called several times to let me know they were coming up short out in Lansing. Still no word from my cousin, which was unlike him. I decided to stop by his crib to see if he was there.

I used the set of keys I had to unlock the door. I stepped in the dark house wit' Jay behind me. Jay cut on the lights while I made my way to the bedroom. The door was closed and I heard the voices of a man and a woman through the door. Opening the door, I scanned the room only to find the voices I heard were comin' from the TV.

When we left Starks' apartment, we rode to my aunt's house to look around then to Kee's house. Cola was nowhere to be found. I was starting to think Zell got to her. The thought of that had me ready to knock down every door in the fuckin' state to find Cola. Zell would kill Cola slow if he got ahold to her.

For three days and three nights, we were all out looking for Cola. Besides a cut off voicemail Starks left me three days ago, we hadn't heard from neither of them. Starks' phone was still going to voicemail. The search for Cola turned into a search for Starks also.

I ain't been to sleep in three days. Ain't ate shit in three days. I wasn't even taking showers. The only thing on my mind was finding Co and my lil ones that were on the way. My heart beat for that girl and my kids. Not knowing where she was and if she cool was fuckin' wit' me bad.

On the morning of the fourth day, everybody was standing in the driveway talking before we went out to look for them again when Starks' car pulled up. I couldn't see anything through his tinted windows. Starks opened his door, that's when I caught a glimpse of Cola sitting in the passenger's seat. I was thankful and pissed off at the same time. Fuck she doing wit' him? How she get wit' him?

"Man I been calling you for a few days. Where you find her at?" I asked Starks calmly. It was hard to keep my cool.

"I tried to call you the night I saw her. She broke my phone before I could tell you I saw her." Starks held up what used to be his iPhone. The front and back of the phone was shattered.

"That don't explain where the fuck y'all been." Jay's superior tone had all eyes glued to Starks. "Three days! For three days we been out here looking for you muthafuckas! Couldn't neither one of y'all find a phone to let us know y'all was good?" Jay yelled.

"Be cool, Jay," I said to him before I continued talking to Starks. "Where was y'all at?" Starks has always been reserved and laid back. It came easy for him to keep his focus on me and disregard Jay.

"Serenity wouldn't come back here. I took her to a hotel to cool off for the night. She wouldn't leave the room for nothing until today." It took me by surprise when Starks called Cola by her real name. She never told anybody her government name. Only the people she was very close to and her family knew what her real name was. What I saw on the video and Starks knowing her real name was suspect to me. A lot was going through my mind about those two things. Shit made me wonder.

"A muthafuckin' hotel!" Jay yelled. Big Curt walked Jay down the driveway to diffuse things before things got out of hand between Jay and Starks.

"Everybody was stressing thinking Zell did somethin' to y'all. Meanwhile, y'all relaxing at the hotel like shit sweet out here. A muthafucka' after us and y'all somewhere chillin'," I said letting my frustration show. The more I thought about this shit the madder I got. One of them could have used the phone at the hotel or somethin'.

"Baker, if you wasn't fuckin' my so called best friend I wouldn't have been in the hotel with your cousin," Cola said as she got out of Starks' car. She pointed to Kee, "Wait until I have these babies bitch. You got a nice ass whoopin' coming to you."

"What the fuck you talking about?" I frowned.

"I heard you and Kee talking that night about if I was gon' be mad about you and her. I hate you, Baker. All the bitches in the world and you fuck her," Cola yelled before she threw her engagement ring in the bushes.

I stared at Cola wit' fire in my eyes. "One day you gon' learn to communicate. You do know yo' brother was in the room right?" I shook my head at the fact that she thought it was me fuckin' around wit' Kee. I haven't cheated on this damn girl not once. Even before shit was official, I wasn't fuckin' wit' no other female.

"I know he was in there. I swear I hate all three of you muthafuckas. Jay you supposed to be my blood and you in there laughing with him," Cola pointed to me. "And that bitch," she pointed at Kee.

"Jay is the one that's fuckin' Kee. You always jumping to some fucked up conclusion about shit. I found out they were together a while back. We was in there talking about telling you and if you would be mad about us keeping the shit from you. Sometimes you make me question yo' thought process."

Cola stood there wit' her arms folded in front of her. Jay explained everything about that night to Cola. Kee wouldn't talk to her because it was the second time she accused her of somethin' she didn't do. Starks told me he stayed wit' her in the hotel because he didn't want to let her out of his sight. He talked her into going out for a drive this morning and brought her here.

After we were all back in the house, I went to the bedroom. Kira came in and handed me the ring Cola threw. I held it between my fingertips and looked at it. The fact that this ring was off her finger over some dumb shit made me question our relationship.

I tossed the ring back to Kira. "I don't want this shit. You can have it."

"I'm cool, Baker. I'm sure you gon' give it back."

"I ain't giving her shit back. She don't deserve it. On top of her throwing it, she was laid up in a hotel wit' my fuckin' cousin, Kira."

"Baker, you can't possibly think some shit popped off wit' them in the hotel. Starks is like a brother to you and Cola love you more than she love herself. You trippin' if you think they would play you like that."

"Cola is unreasonable at times. I don't put shit past her when she all in her feelings."

"Boy, you know damn well ain't nothin' happen between them. Eventually, you will come around. If not, give the ring to Londyn when she gets older." Kira dropped the ring on the bed before she left my room.

I put a lot of thought and money into that ring and Cola gon' toss the muthafucka like that. She ain't ready to get married or ready for a relationship. She needs to be single. The minute she think somethin', she gon' be ready to throw another nigga in my face or do some other stupid shit.

Back in the day, when my mama and pops had issues they talked through that shit. When my mama thought somethin' you better believe she had pops at the kitchen table or in the bedroom asking him about it. I wish Co could be like that instead of doing stupid shit like this when she assumed somethin'.

Cola came in the room looking embarrassed. "Baker I'm sorry. I heard Kee talking to you, well it seemed like she was talking to you. The way it sounded was like you and her had something going on. I love you. I don't wanna lose you." She picked up the ring off the bed; I snatched it before she could put it on her finger. "I can't have my ring back?"

"Nah and you just lost me."

"Over this stupid stuff? Seriously, Baker. You just gon' abandon me and your kids over something petty like this?"

"Now, it's stupid. Was it stupid when you had yo' ass laid up in a hotel? I was losing my fuckin' mind over you being gone. Not knowing if somethin' happened to you or not. It wasn't petty when you threw the ring in the bushes? You ain't ready for it. I ain't abandoning my kids. I'mma always spend time wit' and take care of my lil ones."

"Baker my emotions all over the place. It sounded like you and her were keeping something from me."

"Maybe you right about how things sounded to you. Instead of asking me what was up, you chose to come to yo' own conclusion."

"Baby, you know what I've been through in the past."

"By all means, I tried to show you somethin' different from what you dealt wit' in the past. I never strayed outside our relationship or shit, yet you still accuse me of it. Out of all the women in Chicago, you think I would pick Kee? Yo' best friend. Fuck I look like doing some shit like that?" Cola was frustrating me wit' her bullshit excuses. Instead of her just saying she fucked up, she was trying to justify her actions. I wasn't going for that shit.

"I'm sorry."

"A'ight.

"You forgive me?"

"Yep."

"Can I have the ring now?"

"Nope."

"Baker, baby—"

"Look, I don't have nothing more to say about it. This ring didn't mean shit to you when you took it off. You shouldn't miss it."

Leaving Cola was the hardest thing I ever had to do in life. It hadn't even been thirty minutes, and I missed her ass already. I loved that girl wit' everything in me, but she needed to be taught a lesson. Cheating was one thing I could never do to her. My pops instilled that in me at a young age. Maybe this time apart would teach her to think before she acted.

I got my mind right about Cola prior to going to see if Big Curt had audio on his security system, unfortunately, he didn't. He already knew why I wanted to know that. We all saw Starks grab Cola's arm on the tape. It was evident he wanted to talk to her. Only the two of them will know about what. My gut was telling me some bullshit was going on.

Quite a few thoughts were racing through my mind about Cola and Starks. Unlike Cola, I didn't let what I thought control my actions. My O.G. used to tell me what was done in the dark always came to light. Over the years, I found that to be very true. Until somethin' about Cola and Starks came to light, there was no need for me to dwell on the shit.

Sitting in the room wasn't doing nothing for me besides making me think about the wrong shit. I followed the sound of everybody's voices to the backyard. Goo had exactly what I needed in his hand, a blunt. As soon as I sat next to him, he passed me the blunt. Wit' every hit I took, the stress faded away.

"You good, Baker?"

"I left her ass, Goo."

"What? You and Cola is the reason all of us are in relationships. We all trying to have what y'all have. Remember how I used to cheat on Kira? Had her fighting and trying to kill me."

"How could I forget that? She was about to blow yo' dick off one day."

"My baby crazy. That ain't the point though. The point is you sat me down and told me to chill out because one day she will leave me for good. I didn't listen to you until I came home one night, and Kira was on the phone talking to Cola about me. I never told you what Kira said to Cola."

"What she say to her?" I was curious to know.

"She said she wished she had a man like you. That made me step my shit up. It's still a work in progress for me. In two years, I've only cheated with three chicks. Coming from a nigga that had a new chick with him every week that deserves some type of award."

"That's what's up, Goo. I could understand if Cola went through wit' me what Kira go through wit' you, but she don't. Other than minor arguments and the time I fucked up and disrespected her, she ain't went through shit wit' me. I make sure she don't need or want for shit, Goo. Cola has been trippin' ever since she been dealing wit' Zell. This what she wanted to do. If she couldn't handle it, she should've let me do it the way I wanted to." I hit the blunt again. Co was stressing me the fuck out bad. If I weren't already bald, I wouldn't have no hair fuckin' wit' her.

"I hear you homie. Are you absolutely sure you done?"

"No decision is permanent. I love, Cola, but I ain't one of them soft sucka ass niggas. She need to know I will leave her ass if she keeps on," I said before I passed Goo the blunt.

"I feel you on that. I hope y'all work it out."

We sat in the backyard and smoked the night away. Jay was back and forth between the backyard and the house checking on Cola. Jay understood why I did what I did. Even he talked to Cola about solely going off what she thinks.

Half of my night was spent outside listening to everybody talk shit and smoking. At some point, we ended up telling old stories from the past. Going back down memory lane took my mind off everything until I went in the house to my bedroom. I wanted to check on Cola, but I had to maintain my position.

Throughout the next day, I acted like I didn't know Cola; she did the same to me. Jay was trying to get Cola in a better mood. She was walking around wit' swollen red eyes, and her hair was a mess. She would only speak when spoken to. If she heard my voice in the same room as her, she would get up and leave.

Later that afternoon, my guys and me were all in Big Curt's backyard playing basketball. He had a half-sized court that we played on whenever we got a chance. Through all the shit talk, I heard Kimmy calling my name from the door.

I jogged over to her, and Kira was standing. I picked my shirt up off the chair I left it on and used it to wipe the sweat off my face, "What up doe?"

"Cola won't eat."

"Maybe she ain't hungry, Kimmy."

"The babies need food." Kimmy had her hands on her hips. Kira was right next to her giving me the evil eye.

"Cola, not gon' starve them." I turned to go back to the court to finish the game.

I felt a hand smack the back of my head. "Baker if you don't get yo' bald headed ass in there and make her eat I'mma split yo' shit wide the fuck open." All I could do was laugh at Kira. I knew she would really try to carry out that threat or die trying.

"Kira, I ain't scared to press charges on yo' crazy ass."

"Go in there and make her eat," Kira said. I could hear Goo laughing on the court from where I was standing.

"Chill, Kira," Goo shouted.

Kira yelled, "You shut yo' short ass up. This don't have shit to do wit' you. Please don't get me started on you Goo. Please don't make me do it." Kira stomped her foot on the ground letting Goo know she was ready for him. They had one funny ass relationship.

"Okay, Kira, I'm shutting up. When you leave I'mma start talking again." Everybody laughed when Goo mimicked Smokey off Friday.

Kira turned her attention back to me. "You still here?"

"I'm going muthafucka'. For the record if she wasn't pregnant I wouldn't do nothing."

Cola was sitting on the couch looking at somethin' in her phone. She must have heard me coming because she looked up, curled her top lip up, and looked right back at her phone. That look didn't faze me, so I kept on walking towards her. But if looks could kill, I would be dead.

I pulled my shorts up on my waist and sat right beside her. I studied her face before I said anything to her. Her eyes were still kind of puffy from crying. I felt bad as hell for being the reason for her tears, but some shit just needed to be done. Cola looked over at me and rolled her eyes before she looked back at her phone.

"They told me you won't eat. I know you upset and probably don't wanna eat, but you need to eat for our boys."

Cola got up without saying a word to me and came back wit' a plate of Spaghetti. "I don't need you to tell me to eat."

"Well, tell yo' girls don't come running to me when you ain't doing somethin'. I just came to check on you.'

"I don't need you to check on me either."

"To be honest, it ain't you I'm worried about. My kids are my main concern, if you ain't eating that mean they ain't eating. Regardless to what's going on wit' us right now you still have to think about them."

"Like you care about them."

"Don't pull that you don't care shit wit' me, Co. You made things like this when you took the ring off."

"That ring meant everything to me. I thought it didn't mean anything to you."

"That's the problem right there. Either you don't think or you overthink."

"You kill me acting like you can do no wrong. Like you don't make mistakes," Cola snapped at me.

"Never said I didn't. Be clear on this, I'm not the one that messed our relationship up, you did. You can't be mad at nobody but yourself. I ain't trying do this back and forth thing wit' you right now. Can you eat so I can go on about my business?" Giving Cola this treatment was killin' me. I know I can't keep this up much longer.

Hours later she was done wit' her food. She purposely ate slow just to make me sit there wit' her. I didn't say a word to her. It would only lead to an argument. I wasn't the arguing type of nigga, so I just sat there patiently waiting on her to finish eating.

Before I got up, my Aunt Carla called me and put Londyn on the phone. My baby girl was having the time of her life out in Cali. The sound of her voice made me wish I was there wit' her. She told me she missed me and wanted me to come see her. I wished I could hop on a plane and go have some fun wit' my lil lady. That lil girl meant everything to me.

I watched Cola walk away wit' her head down. I knew she was about to cry again. I still had to stand my ground a lil longer. Her looking all sad was getting to me though. I was weak for this damn girl. I wasn't scared to admit that shit to nobody.

Whenever she hurt, I hurt. Maybe she would stop overthinking after this lesson taught her.

Zell

For the past week, I'd been in the hospital tellin' the doctor and nurse I felt weak and dizzy. I had to do somethin' to buy me some time to figure out a plan. When it finally hit me, I patted myself on the back. Baker and the rest of them mufuckas gon' be in for a surprise after this.

It was a miracle the bullet only grazed my head. Baker said I never knew when death would come knockin' at my door. He was right about that. Hearin' the voices of two men that I thought were dead had me shot the fuck out. I was trippin' so hard I didn't see the silver Camaro pull up on the side of me.

The passenger had the window rolled all the way down. This nigga looked me directly in the eyes and a lump formed in my throat. It was the same lil nigga I just saw break into Kee crib. For days, I wondered what the fuck he was after me for. Then it dawned on me that it was a set up the whole time. Baker and the rest of them niggas set that shit up. I couldn't even hate on the shit they do, they good. I couldn't wait to have one up on them after my next stunt.

I was happy it wasn't Starks in the car. He nice wit' the gun. His aim was on point. He never missed unless he wanted to. Starks never hit anyone that wasn't his intended target. If that lil nigga had his skills, most likely the bullet would have ended up in my skull, and I would be dead or fucked up for the rest of my life.

Wasn't no point in paying Starks' mama a visit now. Them comin' at me was a sign that anybody of importance to them was safe and sound somewhere, and I would never find them. That also meant eyes would probably be on me at all times from now on end. They could watch me if they wanted to. I hope they knew I was gonna be ready for their ass.

"Marlene, I need vitals for room six," I heard a doctor say. The nurse came in the room and wrote somethin' down on a small notepad after she checked the machines. The doctor walked in the room, and the nurse told him my vitals were stable and when I wake up she would be changin' my bandage.

"Change the bandage if you need to. I'm up."

She jumped. "You startled me. I'll change it for you right away. Do you need anything?"

"I'm good for right now. Don't I know you?" I asked lookin' in her face tryin' to figure out where I knew her from.

She turned her face away from me. "I don't think so sir."

"I never forget the face of a bitch I fuck. I was wit' you the night I got shot in my chest a few years back. Yeah, that was you. I thought you lived in Atlanta."

Her eyes almost popped out of her head. "Zell?"

"Yeah, that's me." She tensed up when I confirmed who I was. I could feel her hands shake while she was cleanin' the open wound on the side of my head. Her hands trembled as she applied the new bandage. "Why you nervous? Don't you do this every day all day?"

Through a shaky voice she said, "I never expected to see you again that's all. When I got your chart, I didn't know it was you. I am from Atlanta. I moved here a year ago. This is the third time you've gotten shot. You must have a lot of enemies."

"Somethin' like that."

She took her gloves off and tossed them in the garbage. "We're done for right now. Press the button if you need anything."

"I need somethin'."

"What would that be?"

"Yo' number. We need to pick up where we left off. I never got round three that night," I laughed.

"I'll take yours." She handed me her cell phone to put my number in.

"Make sure you use the mufucka'." Her ass swayed from side to side as she left the room. God was good to her in more ways than one.

The next day I stopped fakin' it and let them discharge me. My car was parked in a well-lit area of the hospital's parkin' lot, not that it made a difference. These niggas were ruthless; they shot at me on a busy street full of traffic cameras. I still hadn't found out who the bitch was that shot me on the E-way that day.

Fear was somethin' that I never experienced. No niggas or some unknown bitch could make my heart pump pussy. I only wanted to be aware of my surroundings.

Rows of cars were blockin' my view of my Audi. I popped the locks anyway just in case some shit went down. The white Range Rover that was parked next to mine had its headlights on. That was strange seein' as how it was light outside. It dawned on me that Baker drove a white Range. It had to be him in the car. My .9 was tucked in my waist wit' a full clip. I was ready for whatever.

The closer I got to my car, the more my adrenaline pumped. I squinted my eyes to get a better look inside the car. The sun temporarily blinded me; I couldn't see nothin' from a distance. I put my hand on my pistol when I was only a few cars away from my own car.

The headlights on the car next to mine suddenly went out. Pickin' up speed, I walked to the driver side of my car. When the door to the white Range Rover flew open, I raised my pistol up. The old pale white doctor turned bloodshot red when he saw the gun aimed directly at his head. The doctor ran to the hospital entrance as fast as he could. I tucked my pistol back in my waist and looked around one last time.

As I reached for my door handle, I felt a hand grab my arm. I was about to grab my pistol until I saw who it was. I looked at this bitch like she lost her mind and snatched away from her.

"Clearly you have a problem keeping your mouth shut, Zell."

"Clearly yo' ass has a problem keepin' yo' legs closed," I shot back.

"We had an agreement about what happened between us."

"And? Yo' point is?" I folded my arms across my chest.

"What do you mean and? We both agreed to take what happened to our grave."

"No. You said you would take it to your grave. I said I wouldn't tell nobody. I never said I would keep the shit a secret forever," I smirked. That was the truth. When me and Kee started fuckin', I told her I wouldn't tell nobody. She said she would take it to her grave. I didn't agree to that shit. She didn't have no business standin' in my face tryin' to check me.

"I swear to God I hate you. I shouldn't have tried to help you out. I should have let them kill you. You couldn't even kill Baker like you was supposed to. Now, I can't wait until they get rid of you. Cola won't believe you anyway."

"Kee, you can hate me all you want to. I still fucked you in more ways than one. Once I tell Cola about the tat on yo', ass she will believe me. You simple bitch. So jealous of yo' own friend that you fucked me while me and her was together and got my number out her phone and texted me some info just so I can kill Baker, and she can suffer. Wit' friends like you, who the fuck needs enemies?"

"What makes you think she gon' talk to you?"

"She don't have to talk to me. Text messages are meant to be read. I don't wanna talk to that bitch anyway. She did me dirty, had me thinkin' we were workin' on gettin' back together and whatnot."

"Text her, send a smoke signal, do whatever you want. She still won't believe I fucked you, and she really won't believe I gave you the address." Kee believed every word she just said. I thought it was cute that she was standin' here lookin' all confident.

I laughed, "Yo' short, pretty ass think you know it all. One thing you don't know about is the tape. I got screenshots of the texts you sent me wit' the address." Kee's face fell on the floor when I said that. She didn't look too confident now.

"Tape? What tape?"

"The tape of me and you fuckin' in every position you can think of. I had you moanin' and screamin' for God. Matter of fact, I watched that tape last night. You are one of my top five pieces of pussy. Even though Cola played me she gon' always be number one."

"Fuck you, Zell! If I had a gun, I would kill you myself!" Kee screamed.

"I should kill you right here, right now. Instead, I'mma let you look yo' best friend in the face like you ain't a backstabbin' hoe, bitch. Just for you tryin' to check me I'mma make sure I send Cola some screenshots from the tape and of the texts you sent. I wonder how that will turn out for you. Yo' mama didn't want you, you don't know yo' daddy, and yo' sister that you won't tell Cola you in touch wit' only talk to you when she need you to do somethin' for her. Once Cola sees this, you gon' be all alone in the world. Have a pleasant day now, Kee," I smiled.

Kee stormed off lookin' dumb as hell after she gave me the finger. She knew she couldn't deny what happened now. I had visual evidence of her bein' a slut.

Kee had major balls for comin' to check me. Nobody told her to throw it at me. Like any nigga would, I caught it. Wit' her bein' Cola's friend I had to record her. I didn't know if it was some type of trap or what. If it was a trap, I was gon' expose that bitch to the hood. Turns out all she wanted to do was experience the dick Cola was gettin'.

When I got them texts from her talkin' about getting' rid of Baker, I wasn't shocked. Kee had always been jealous of Cola. She was jealous of Cola's relationship wit' her mother, brother, me, and now Baker.

Kee used to go on and on about how Cola got everything handed to her while she had to work hard for everything. Cola never had to work because the niggas in her life always took care of her. Kee secretly hated her best friend. She didn't even tell Cola that she got in touch wit' her long lost sister right before Cola lost her baby. She had Cola 'nim thinking she didn't know where that bitch was at.

I used to have a little respect for Kee before she crossed Cola like that. The thought of fuckin' Kee never even crossed my mind before she came at me. The same bitch that ran to the hospital after Cola lost that baby and snapped on me at Baker's picnic is the same bitch that was fuckin' me behind her back.

What Cola don't know was, when Kee approached me at the picnic, she wasn't mad because I disrespected Cola. She was mad because I fucked her the day before while Cola was gettin' a check-up. Kee tried to trip about me bein' out wit' another bitch like she was my girl or some shit. She was there wit' her man anyway. These hoes be crazy.

I was out and about like shit was cool in the streets. You would think niggas wasn't out to get me the way I was out in the open. Wit' the stunt Kee pulled, I knew they wasn't watching me. She wouldn't have stepped to me if they had eyes on me. I stopped at Cain's Barber College on 51st Street to get a fresh cut before my date wit' Marlene tonight.

When I finally made it home, I sat down to write a short letter to Anaya's uncle. I went over the letter to make sure I got my point across before I sealed the envelope. I used my phone to look up his information then copied it to the envelope. Before I met with Marlene, I had to stop at the mailbox to drop the letter in. I needed to get the ball rollin' on this. I couldn't wait to see how this shit played out.

At seven on the dot, I met Marlene at the lakefront. She had on a long, blue dress, some blue thong sandals, and a blue jean jacket. Her curly hair was blowin' in the wind. The blue flower she had in her hair made me think I was in Hawaii or somethin'. She was lookin' real good.

"Hey Dezell." She smiled when I walked up to her.

"Stop callin' me Dezell." I hated my real name. I was named after a nigga that I didn't know. My hoe of a mother didn't even know the nigga name. So I know she ain't know what the nigga looked like.

"I'm sorry, Zell." Marlene guided me towards the concrete steps where a few other people were sittin' actin' all lovey dovey. Kissin' and huggin' and all that bullshit. Corny ass mufuckas.

Marlene and me sat down on the concrete steps. "Let me ask you somethin'. You saw my medical records right?"

"Yes, I have to see them."

"So you know what the doctor said I got right?"

"Yes, I know what you have. I know what you're wondering. I gave you my number because I don't discriminate. I give people chances. If I like you enough, I'll accept everything you come with," Marlene smiled.

"You must have read my mind. That's exactly what I was thinkin' about."

"I figured as much. Let's walk further down. My brothers are in town for our mom's birthday. I told them I would stop by here for a second. That's why I wanted to meet here."

"Aight man." I didn't wanna meet these people on the first date. I didn't wanna meet them mufuckas at all.

We walked towards a crowd of niggas standin' around drinkin' and talkin'. All eyes were on me when I got closer to the crowd. I assumed the two that were lookin' at me extra hard were her brothers.

Marlene introduced us to each other. "Zell, these are my big brothers, Trell and Maine."

"What up?" they said in unison. They didn't look shit like her. She had an exotic look like she was mixed or somethin'. They looked like straight up niggas.

"Shit chillin'. What's up wit' y'all?"

"Come here, Marlene," Maine said. They walked away leavin' me and Trell standin' there.

"Yo' sister told me y'all don't stay here. Where y'all from?"

"Philly." He had a frown on his face when he answered my question.

Trell never took his eyes off of me while we were standing there. Wasn't no use in tryin' to talk to him. I could tell by the look on his face he wasn't gon' say much of nothin'. Fuck him. I wasn't into small talk anyway. I took this opportunity to send Cola those screenshots of the tape.

I would hold on to the screenshots of the texts for now. Marlene made her way back to me as soon as I pressed send. I would love to be a fly on the wall to see what happened between Cola and Kee when this shit hit the fan.

"Aye my man," Maine said as he stood next to Marlene. "Little sis just gave me the rundown on you. What type of beef you got? If my sister gon' be out here with you, she needs to be safe."

"Minor shit that I can handle. I don't need yo' sister tellin' you my business." I looked over at Marlene wit' a look that let her know she shouldn't have told my fuckin' business. She turned her head to avoid makin' eye contact wit' me.

Trell interrupted, "No need for the hostilities."

Maine continued, "Relax; I'm about to offer a helping hand. Guns, bullets, vests, silencers. I got bombs if you need them jawns."

"At what cost?" This shit sounded too good to be true. It had to be a catch to it.

Trell looked at Marlene and said, "Her safety."

Maine nodded, "Anything happens to her, Chicago won't be on the map nomo'. I recommend you take me up on my offer to get the proper artillery to handle that problem you have."

"Yo' offer sound good and all, but I can't help but think it's too good to be true."

"Trust me it's all for Marlene. Take my number and give me a call within a week. On the assumption that you will call, I'll have a few things waiting for you."

I programmed Maine's number in my phone. I probably would call him. I was a one man army out here. I was gonna need more than the two guns I had. My .44 stayed in my car, and my .9 stayed on my waist. I needed one for every room in my crib just in case them niggas tried to run up in there on me.

Marlene wanted to stay wit' her brothers. I stayed wit' her for a few hours and talked to Maine; he was cool people. Trell was the one that I didn't like. Nigga didn't say much, just watched me.

Marlene told me to make sure I called Maine and don't think too much of Trell. She said he like that wit' any man that come around her. I walked to my car to go home. Surprisingly when I pulled off it still wasn't nobody followin' me. Shit must be about to get real. I pulled out my phone and set up the meet wit' Maine for later this week. I was gonna be war ready when the time came.

Cola

Five long days. That was how long Baker and I had been broken up. We were under the same roof and we past each other like strangers for the most part. The only time we spoke was if Londyn called one of us, or when he checked on the babies. The thought of this being permanent broke my heart.

I felt like he took his gun and shot me in the heart. It hurts so bad to lose the person that made your day and completed you. Every time I heard a knock on my bedroom door I hoped it was him, when it was not I was disappointed. When my phone rang, I rushed to it praying that he was calling or texting me from the other side of the house.

I wished I could take back everything that happened that night. It was so stupid of me to stay in a hotel with Starks knowing Baker would probably think Zell got to me. I prayed Starks stayed true to his word and never told Baker about what happened between us at the hotel. We already had a secret past that we were keeping from him. I felt so bad about not telling him. I didn't wanna lose him.

No Ordinary Love by Sade was turned up to the max coming through my Beats. I felt exactly what she was saying in the song. Sade was talking for me at the moment. I had it on repeat for what seemed like forever. Usually, when I was going through a breakup Kee was right next to me going through it with me. I needed my best friend back as soon as possible. I snatched my headphones out of my ear, picked up my phone, and went to find Kee.

Everybody was sitting around in the living room except for Kee and Jay. I spoke to everyone as I past them. They were all surprised to see me out of my room. I mostly only came out to use the bathroom or to eat. Kira asked me how I was doing and rubbed my round belly. It seemed to pop out overnight. Baker never took his eyes off of me as I walked through the room. It took all the willpower I had in me not to say anything to him.

Kee's door was closed when I approached her room. I could hear her and Jay arguing about something. When I heard Jay's voice get louder than hers, I tapped on her door.

Kee yelled, "Who is it?"

"It's Cola. I need to talk to you, Kee."

The door flung open, and Jay walked out wit' no shirt on and his fists balled up. "Hey sis. You a'ight? I have been worried about you and my nephews. Damn you got big as hell. What you been doing in that room?" Leave it to Jay to make me laugh when I wanted to cry.

"Shut up Jay. And you don't have to worry about me I'm okay. I'll get past this like I get past everything else."

"A'ight then strong black woman," Jay chuckled as he walked away with his fist balled up in the air.

Kee was sitting on the bed looking extremely upset. She stared at me with cold eyes. I knew I was wrong for thinking her and Baker had something going on. I need to start thinking things through like Baker said.

"Kee, I'm so sorry about everything. I should have known you wouldn't do me like that. You have never given me a reason to think you would stab me in the back."

"Apology accepted. I do want to know why you felt the need to call my job. That was low." A couple days ago, I called Kee's job and told them she smoke weed. Sometimes I shook my head at my damn self for the stuff I did. I thought I was a grown woman, but lately I'd been able to see that I really had some growing up to do. Especially if I wanted to keep my family together.

"Anger. Instead of coming to you, I let my anger speak for me."

"At least you honest."

"Did you get fired? I feel so bad." I really did regret calling her job after I did it. Once again, I let my emotions get the best of me.

"I didn't get fired. I had to take a drop on the spot. Luckily, I know somebody that know somebody, and they looked out for me. You could have cost me my job, Cola."

"Thank God. Do you forgive me?" I pouted.

"Of course I forgive you, Co. An apology is all I wanted from you." Kee reached her arms out for a hug. We sat on her bed and embraced each other tightly. I needed that so bad.

"What's wrong?" I asked when I noticed Kee staring into space.

"Jay has been talking to Marlene. We were arguing about that before you came in here. Apparently Zell was her patient after Roc shot him on Western. He recognized her and asked for her number. She texted Jay and told him how scared she was that he was going to kill her, and they've been talking ever since."

"I don't see a problem with that, Kee."

"I'm not finished," she said with a hint of attitude.

"Proceed, Queen Kee."

She let out a faint laugh before she continued, "Jay went to meet her the other night, supposedly to talk. When he got back, he wouldn't fuck me. Me being the type of person I am, I went through his phone after he fell asleep. Marlene sent him a text that I wished I hadn't seen."

"What did the text say?"

"It said, and I quote, we still have the best sex I've ever had in my life. I miss it and you. I want us to get back to the way we were."

"Wow. I'm at a loss for words. Did you ask him about it? Did he respond to the text?"

"No, I haven't asked him about it yet and he responded. He told her he missed her too, and he told her he love her. How he lay up with me every night, but tell the next bitch he loves her?"

I was shocked to hear that Jay told Marlene he loved her. I always knew he liked her, but he never said he loved her. I also knew Jay stayed with Marlene when we first came back to the city from Dekalb. I wasn't about to tell Kee that. The relationship between my best friend and my brother was none of my business. Jay would always be my brother, and I was not throwing him under the bus for nobody.

"Ask him about it, Kee. It's gon' drive you crazy just sitting here thinking about it. Believe me I know."

"I know you know," we both laughed. "You and Baker need to get it together."

"Baker only talks to me about Londyn and checks on me because I'm pregnant. If I wasn't pregnant, he wouldn't say more than three words to me. Things have never been this bad between us. I think it's over for good. Anyway, you need to check Jay about what he did." My phone vibrated in my lap letting me know that I had a text message. I chose to ignore the message for right now. It was more important for me to be there for my best friend.

"Girl, Baker is not about to leave you and let some other man raise his kids. Nor would he be able to stomach another man being with you. It will be a cold day in hell before he leaves you. As far as Jay, I'll ask him when I feel the time is right. I can't believe after all this changing he claimed he's done; he's still up to the same crap." Kee looked like she was fed up. I would be too if I was with a man like my brother. I loved Jay, but he wasn't shit when it came to relationships.

"Hopefully, you're right about Baker. I don't know what to say about Jay."

"He will be single if he keeps playing with me.'

"Girl, please. You know you not going nowhere," I laughed. My phone vibrated again letting me know I had another text message. "What does he want?" I said aloud.

"Who?" Kee frowned as she stood in the mirror taking a good look at herself. I saw her looking at me in the mirror. When I glanced up, she quickly took her eyes off me. She fixed an out of place hair and put on some MAC lipgloss. Sitting back on the bed, she asked again, "What who want Co? Who keep texting you?" Kee was adamant about knowing who was texting me. She even leaned in a little to try to peek at my phone. I was about to ask her if she was expecting a text on my phone. She was a little too thirsty.

"I'll be right back."

Maneuvering through the living room, I quickly walked to my room. I couldn't help but notice the huge smile Kira had plastered on her face when I past her. I shook it off and continued to walk with a quick pace. My legs couldn't move fast enough as I hurried to the other side of the house where my temporary room was located. I looked at my phone once again to make sure my eyes weren't deceiving me.

Anger pulsated through my body when I opened the door to my room. It was like he was toying with my emotions for whatever reason. I flopped down on the bed like I had lost my best friend. My phone reminded me that I had another text. Just as I was about to unlock my phone, Baker walked out of the bathroom located in my room only wearing a towel.

"What up doe?" Baker said when he stepped in the room. His body was still damp, and he looked mouthwatering. I thought back to when I used to dry him off in the bathroom before he left the house. He would always pick me up and put me on the sink afterwards for a shot of morning sex. Then get right back in the shower. I needed my man back.

"I thought you were playing some type of game with me." I was happy Baker was actually in my room like he texted. I was about to find him and curse him out.

"I just took a shower. I need to holla at you right quick," Baker said as he loosened the towel around his waist. He looked me in the eyes as he dried off and got dressed. I wanted so badly to touch him, but I knew better than that. We still weren't back together. I had to keep my hands to myself. He knew what he was doing, and I hated him for him for it.

"About what?" I said like I didn't care what he wanted.

"Maine just called me. He said Zell set up a meet wit' him and Trell. After Marlene told Jay that Zell was her patient, she pretended Trell and Maine were her brothers. They got him thinking he was coming to get some guns. I know you wanted to be there, but the thing is you showing now. If shit gets hectic, he can easily take yo' life and the twins' lives. I can't have you there tonight. I'm thinking about the what ifs. What if he pop you before we can pop him? What if he know we about to dead him and he shoot you or some shit?"

"Yet you tell me I think too much," I rolled my eyes.

"You do. About the wrong shit. I'm thinking about our kids and their mother."

"Don't think for me or about me." I stood to leave the room. I was halted by Baker's deep voice.

"Don't think for you or about you," he chuckled. "Fuck outta here wit' all that. If I didn't think for you or about you, yo' ass would probably still be wit' that nigga sitting in a fuckin' clinic getting pills for HIV. Or crying on Jay or Kee's shoulder about some fucked up shit he did to you."

I stood in the middle of the room with my back towards Baker. Everything he said was true. I couldn't turn around to face him yet. Feeling stupid, I dropped my head in defeat. There was no argument valid enough for me to try to get the last word.

"Think about how you would feel if another woman has to raise Londyn."

I was about to tell him exactly how I would feel about that until my phone alerted me of the texts I never read. My screen said I had six unread messages. Once I opened the first message; my heart skipped a beat. It was a picture of Kee laying in the bed I shared with Zell long ago butt naked.

The second picture was Kee on her knees with Zell's dick in her mouth. The third was her bent over with Zell right behind her. The fourth was her squirting while Zell stood there and watched. Picture number five was Kee riding Zell reverse cowgirl. Last but not least picture number six was Kee with Zell's cum all over her face.

With my mouth wide open, I started to have a panic attack. Baker ran to my side to calm me down until the attack passed. After my breathing returned to normal, I gave Baker my phone. His mouth dropped as he looked at all six pictures. Baker sat me down and held me in his arms. This was what I'd been wanting him to do just not under these circumstances.

When I asked Kee about this, she sat there and lied in my face. That bitch deserved the ultimate ass whoopin' for this. I was so mad; I wasn't even mad. My best damn friend, who was in a relationship with my brother betrayed me in the lowest way possible. In my book, Kee was now my enemy.

"Damn baby I'm so sorry. I'm mad at myself because I stuck up for that bitch in the hospital. Let me make sure this shit official. I wouldn't put it past him to alter the pictures." Baker examined the pictures carefully. "Kee's a trifling ass bitch for this."

"She had me apologizing for accusing her of doing it. All along she did do it. She was laying up with my brother every night like she not a lying ass bitch."

"Man, man, man," Baker said as he shook his head.

"I need to tell Jay. Forward it to his phone for me, then delete the text. I don't want to look at it again. Then I'm going to her room to whoop her ass." I was beyond ready to lay hands on Kee.

"You ain't whoppin' no ass while my lil ones in there, Co. I ain't gon' let that go down. So you can forget about that."

Less than a minute later, Jay came busting in my room with his phone in one hand and his gun in the other. "Where you get these pictures from sis?"

"Zell sent them to me. I got them while I was in there talking to her, but I ignored them. She was telling me she went through your phone and found out you slept with Marlene the other night. I called myself being a good friend and consoled that bitch." I jumped up and bolted towards the door ready to go do damage on Kee. Baker grabbed my arm before I reached the door. Jay blocked the doorway, so I couldn't get out.

Holding both of my arms, Baker spoke in a calm but firm tone, "Chill out wit' all that, Co. You can beat her ass every day if you want to after you have the babies. For now be cool baby."

"Fuck that, Baker! This bitch crossed me, and when I asked her about it, she made me feel guilty about it." Kee had me so mad my brown skin turned red. I wanted to whoop her ass all through this house. I was standing there plotting an escape route to try to get past Baker. He was still holding my arms. I knew he wasn't gon' let me go, so I gave up.

Steam was coming from the top of my head. I couldn't believe Kee did that dirty shit to me. I wasn't hurt about it because it was so long ago. I was mad as hell about the principle of the situation. She supposed to be my best friend, my sister, my confidant. It was crazy because I never even suspected she was messing with Zell behind my back. I couldn't wait to drop this load so I could serve her a nice ass whoopin'.

"Now, I'm glad I fucked Marlene. I was starting to feel bad about that. Matter of fact, y'all just act like everything is normal wit' her. I got somethin' lovely for her," Jay said as he pulled his phone out. Baker and I listened to Jay's conversation. "What's up wit' it?....What time you get off?....I have been thinking about you since the other night....Come see me tonight when you get off.....Hit me before you leave so I can give you the address.....Don't trip you ain't gotta miss me no longer." Jay displayed an evil smile as he hung his phone up.

"What you got up yo' sleeve bruh?" Baker asked with a raised eyebrow.

"A lil payback for that big head broad. She lucky I don't beat bitches," Jay said through clenched teeth.

I was in my own world while Jay and Baker were talking. Jay asked me to pretend like everything was normal. That was gon' be hard to do. How could I smile in her face like we were friends when I didn't even trust her? Whatever Jay has planned, I hope it hurts her soul.

Jay left my room, and Baker stayed back. He grabbed my hand and pulled me up off the bed. He rubbed my stomach before pulling me close to him. He squeezed me like it was the last time he would touch me again. I didn't know what was on his mind, but I laid my head on his chest and savored the moment.

Baker took one arm from around me and lifted my chin up. He leaned in to give me one of those passionate kisses that made my body shake. After he had kissed me, he undressed me and gently laid me on the bed. Baker kissed my body from head to toe before he got undressed and got in the bed with me.

No words were said as we made up. Our bodies did all of the talking for us. I had never experienced a love like this before. This man of mine was a different breed from the rest. To say I loved Baker was an understatement. No word could describe what I felt for him. He was my world, and if I didn't want my world to fall apart, I had some serious changing to do.

Jay

"Shit girl," I said out of breath as I came for the second time in what seemed like five minutes. This some good ass pussy. I didn't feel like fighting the nut like I normally would when we fucked, so I let it go. She was the only woman that could say she made me tap out.

"You know you owe me right?" She laid her head on me and rubbed her fingers across my sweaty chest. "I didn't get mine and you know how I am when I feel cheated."

Licking my lips, I said, "Get up here and get it then." She snatched the covers off me and rode me like I had the last dick on Earth. My dick worked differently from other niggas. I only needed minutes to recover after I let one go. That was one of the reasons all my women loved me. The other reason was, shit, I'm me.

"Ohhh, Jay I'm about to cum." Her hips moved in a fast, circular motion until her body began to shake. "You still the only man that can make me cum," she whispered before she hit the peak of her orgasm.

Both of my hands were on her waist while I stabbed her pussy violently. Her loud moans let me know she was on the verge of another orgasm. The second her body began to shake, my room door flew open. Already knowing who it was, I quickly pulled Marlene closer to me before she could see the light from the door opening. I kissed her neck and squeezed her ass like nobody was standing there.

"Really Jay?" Kee asked wit' her hands on her hip. Marlene hurried to cover herself at the sound of Kee's voice. I folded my hands behind my head and covered myself wit' the sheet.

"What's up wit' it, Kee? You remember Marlene right?" Kee gave me that are you serious look. Marlene was embarrassed, but she waved at Kee anyway. She had no idea what was going on. I knew I would have to explain things to her after it was over. I planned on keeping Marlene around anyway. She put her life on the line for me more than once. She earned a top spot in my life.

"Wow. I sleep in this bed with you every night. And you have the audacity to have a bitch in here." Kee put her hands on her hips.

"Jay, are you with her?" Marlene asked while she started to put her clothes on. She pulled her hair into a ponytail never breaking eye contact wit' me while I slipped my boxers and jeans on.

"I was wit' her until now." I looked at Kee whose facial expression turned from hurt to mad in seconds. I didn't give a fuck about her feelings at all.

"Was? When did it become was? I just woke up with your dick inside of my mouth this morning," Kee yelled wit' tears forming in her eyes.

"Wow, Jay?" Marlene said as she walked towards the door. Kee moved over, so she could exit the room. I was glad they didn't come to blows. I didn't know who would have won that battle. Kee had the most hurtful look on her face when I started to plead wit' Marlene not to leave.

"You begging her not to leave? Unbelievable!" The loudness of Kee's voice made everybody in the house run to see what was going on. Cola and Baker were the first two to arrive. Baker had a smirk on his face as he held Cola in his arms. "How could you do this to me, Jay?"

"The same way you played my sister."

Kee looked at Cola confused. "I haven't done shit to her."

"Save that shit, Kee. You fucked Zell in her bed. Try to lie if you want to. We got proof of that shit." Marlene was trying to jerk away from me. I knew she felt used. I decided to add insult to Kee's injury. I turned to Marlene. "Marlene, I ain't letting you go. We gon' talk and work it out. I have been thinking about you so much man you just don't know. Even when I was fuckin' her I was thinking about you. Why you think I didn't hesitate to come see you the other day? I wanna be wit' you not her." I kissed Marlene on the cheek before she went back in the bedroom.

"Cola, I'm so sorry. It wasn't like that. It just happened," Kee started to plead her case.

Kira spoke before Cola could, "Bitch save that cliché it just happened shit and say what it really was. I think it was you fucked yo' best friend's man. Talking about some damn it just happened. Bitch I should kill you for saying that stupid shit. That don't make no damn sense. Can't trust the bitch that's like a sister to you."

Kira walked up to Kee, pulled a .22 from somewhere and pointed it at her. Kee closed her eyes thinking Kira was about to pop her. After a few seconds, Kee opened her eyes. Kira maintained her stance. "You got twenty minutes to get the fuck up outta here before I put multiple holes in you. That's my word. You bum ass bitch."

Scared, Kee turned to Cola wit' a stream of tears running down her face. "Cola, I should have admitted what I did."

Baker had Cola in a tight hug. He knew if he let her go it was over wit'. "Keep that shouda, woulda, coulda shit to yourself, Kee. I don't want to hear that at all. You did the one fuckin' thing I never felt the need to tell you not to do. That was supposed to be an unspoken rule between us. You had no business in my bed with Zell. I swear if he wasn't holding me I would beat yo' backstabbing hoe ass." Cola grabbed Baker's arm and went back to their room. From the way they were hugged up, I could tell they worked it out.

Kimmy added, "Hurry up and get out of my damn house."

Nobody saw Cola coming when she ran up on Kee. Co hit her dead in the eye. Kee was dazed just from that one hit. Co started giving Kee the business without pulling hair and scratching like most females do. Fuck Mayweather. Co was looking like Cola Ali or somebody. She was quick wit them hands. Kee landed a couple good ones, but Cola was answering right back wit' hard blows that could be heard in the next room.

Kee had a hold on Cola's hair when Baker came rushing out of the room. Despite that, Co was still fuckin' Kee up. Baker tried to pry Cola's hair out of Kee's hand. When he saw Kee trying to kick Cola in the stomach, he pulled his .45 out and pressed it against Kee's temple.

"You might wanna calm the fuck down before shit get uglier than what it is right now." Kee let Cola's hair go and begged Baker not to kill her. Baker took his gun off Kee and looked at Cola wit' fire in his eyes. "Damn Co! I go take a piss and this what you do! You fuckin' pregnant! All y'all standing here letting her humbug again while she pregnant!" None of us said a word. We knew we shouldn't have let that fight go down. Kee deserved that shit though.

"Fuck that! I might not get the chance to whoop that ass after I have my babies! I had to get it out the way now! Dirty bitch!" Cola yelled before she spit at Kee. That there was a sign of pure disrespect.

"Let's go," Baker said in a firm tone while holding on to Cola's arm as they walked to the room. The door slammed shut, and I could hear them arguing about the fight.

"You got a couple knots on yo' head. Try witch hazel for that. Take care, Kee," I said as I waved bye to Kee. She stood there wiping blood from her mouth and feeling the knots Cola left on her head.

"Mark my words you will see me again Jay! You and that bitch Cola! I promise you that!" That was the last thing she screamed before Kira pushed her out the door.

"Yeah a'ight," I waved her off.

Kee got in her car and drove off. East Bumblefuck could have been her destination for all I cared as long as she stayed away from my sister. I vowed to keep all snakes away from Cola. I didn't care who it was. Kee was no exception. To think, I actually gave a fuck about her. I thought about letting all my other women go for her. I was glad I came to my senses and kept them around. If not I would be on the prowl for some new ones.

When I entered the room, Marlene was sitting on the edge of the bed on the phone. She hung up when I sat next to her. Her leg wouldn't stop shaking. She only did it when she was mad. The way her leg was moving almost had me scared to get close to her.

Marlene looked at me wit' a face I never saw her wear. "Did you have to use me like this, Jay? Anytime you have needed me to do something for you I've done it. All you had to do was give me a heads up."

"My fault about all that. It wasn't my intention to make you feel used. I knew what it would do to Kee to see me wit' you. On some real shit, I didn't think about how you would feel when it all unfolded. Only thing I had on my mind was getting back at Kee." That was the truth. The only thing on my mind was revenge. I didn't think about Marlene's feelings.

"Is she the reason you broke things off with me?" Marlene was the type that wanted the truth then got mad when you gave it to her. I was a lil' reluctant to tell her the truth at first. I went ahead and gave her the real.

"Honestly, she is." Marlene got up; I pulled her back down. "Hear me out. Me and her had been off and on for a long time. I thought she was who I wanted to settle down wit'. My heart was wit' her for a nice lil' minute, then all of a sudden I started to think about you a lot. If she really had my heart, I wouldn't have been on that wit' you the other night. I would have done what I had to do to protect you, and that's it."

"Why didn't you tell me about her?"

"Damn, you ask a lot of questions," I laughed along wit' her. "I don't have an answer to that question. So, what's up we gon' try this again or what?"

"Let me think about that. You left me for another woman; she wasn't what you thought you wanted; you used me to make her jealous, now you want me back? That's a lot for me to digest.

I need to sleep on it." Marlene grabbed her car keys off the bed. I snatched them out of her hand to keep her from leaving.

"Sleep on it in my bed." I winked at her and put her keys in my pocket.

Marlene smiled, "That's not fair. That gives you all night to convince me to give you another chance."

I smiled a wide smile at her, "That's what I'm trying to do."

In the middle of the night, I had Marlene screaming that she was gon' fuck wit' me. I loved her, but I really loved Kee. Since she out the picture for good, Marlene was back in it. I didn't look at her different after she fucked Zell all those years ago.

I asked her if she was willing to do whatever it took to get the job done. She said she was, and that was exactly what she did. Marlene risked everything for me when she shot Zell. The least I could do was see where things would go wit' her.

I made sure she didn't fuck him this go round. I don't want either one of us walking around wit' that package Peachy got him carrying around. I wondered what was up wit' Peachy and Tara. The last Baker told me about them; they moved down to Alabama.

After being up all night wit' Marlene, I walked her to the door so she could go home and change for work. Rest was somethin' I needed bad. Otherwise, I would be too tired for the big night. I drifted off into a deep sleep as soon as my head hit the pillow.

Around seven in the evening, Cola woke me up and told me to start getting ready. We talked for about twenty minutes. She told me her and Baker worked everything out and got back together. I told her about Marlene and me.

Cola was cool wit' me talking to Marlene even though she was the one in the bed wit' Zell when Cola finally left him. Cola didn't know it was Marlene that night until me and Baker told her everything. She didn't care since her and Marlene never had much of a relationship. Plus she was already deep in it wit' Baker when that shit went down.

At eight that night, we all were sitting around waiting on Trell and Maine to call and let us know they were at the abandoned school on 38th and State Street. Zell was supposed to meet them there at one in the morning. Starks pulled up at about 8:20 dressed in all white. He said he always wore white when he killed a nigga because he was sending God an angel.

Baker's phone rang at close to nine. It was Trell letting him know we could be on our way to the city. A nigga was excited about putting Zell in the dirt. The thought alone made my dick hard. I said a prayer for God to watch over us and opened the back passenger's door to Goo's black BMW.

Big Curt and Baker were in Big Curt's Bentley. Starks, Jake, and Bubba rode in Jake's white S class Benz. Kira passed me a blunt as we peeled out of the driveway. I put on my red baseball gloves and loaded up while Goo drove us to put our plan in motion.

Zell

I had to get to this school early to check out the scenery. These Philly niggas might be up to no good. I was supposed to be there at one, but I was gonna go around eleven just to make sure wasn't no bullshit goin' on. I had time to smoke and have a few shots before I left. At this time of night, it should only take me less than twenty minutes to get there.

"Damn ain't nowhere for me to park and get a full view of this bitch," I said to myself while I drove down State Street lookin' for a spot to park in. Havin' no other option, I drove around the school every ten minutes to make sure nothin' strange was goin' on.

At 12:30, a red Impala pulled up to the school. I watched as Maine and Trell unloaded four big ass duffle bags from the trunk of the car. They both had looked around cautiously before they entered the old school. Trell came back out of the school and parked on the East side of State Street. He exited the car wit' somethin' that looked like some type of light.

At one on the dot, I got out of my car and walked towards the school. Maine moved a board that was covering the door so he could let me in the school.

"Let me get you to the light," Maine said as he used the light from his cell phone to guide us through the darkness of the school.

"All this space in here and y'all pick the room all the way on the back."

"This is how we do our business. It's hard to find anybody if they all the way back here," Maine explained.

Trell was sittin' in a chair in the dim light wit' dozens of weapons spread out on a sheet he had spread across the floor. I stood close to the doorway and took in the sight in front of me. I was in gun heaven.

"So you don't want no money for these? This shit seem fishy," I frowned.

"I'm giving you the jawns for free because my sister like you. Whatever problem you have you need to get it taken care of. If something happen to Marlene, something gon' happen to you. Believe that," Maine warned. He must think I gave a fuck about his silly ass threat.

"Ain't shit gon' happen to yo' mufuckin' sister. Shit ain't even that major," I said as I eyed the guns. I already had my top six picks.

Trell leaned forward in the chair he was sittin' in. "Take your pick."

Lookin' down at the guns, I focused on the ones that caught my eye. The small shit wasn't what I was after. I wanted the big shit for Jay and Baker specifically. I grabbed the AR-15, M4 and some shit that I didn't know the name of. It was big but light in weight.

It had to be some military shit that I've never heard of. I was gonna use this one on Baker's pussy ass when the time came. When I asked them what the lil cord on the bottom was, they said it was nothin' important and that I made a good choice by pickin' it.

"That's all you want?" Maine asked when he handed me a duffle bag.

"Hell yeah. This more than enough. If I only pull the trigger on one of these, I know it will eliminate them mufuckas for good." I put the unzipped bag on my shoulder and headed towards the exit. I put my hand in the bag and put my finger on the trigger of the unknown weapon while I walked through the darkness of the school. I didn't know these niggas; they might be on some other shit. If they were, I'd be ready to put some heat in their ass.

Outside of the school, the air felt funny. I had a feelin' somethin' was about to go down. I popped the trunk of my car, put my old guns and two of my new guns inside and closed the trunk. The only one I kept out was the unknown gun. I only took one step before I felt cold steel pressed against the back of my head. I wasn't worried about shit. I had some serious artillery in my hand. Whoever this nigga was didn't know what's about to happen to him.

"Turn around," the voice said. I slowly turned around to see Goo pointin' a .44 at me. "Drop that shit."

"I ain't droppin' shit. It's gon' be me or you tonight," I said in a confident tone.

Goo laughed before he lowered his gun. "A'ight then shoot me and see what happens."

Wit' no hesitation I shot Goo right in the chest. When I saw a red splatter on his shirt, I knew he was gon' fall in a matter of seconds. To my surprise, he didn't. My eyes almost popped out of my socket when I took a good look at his shirt. Them niggas gave me a fuckin' paintball gun. My nostrils flared when Goo started laughin'.

"Ain't this a bitch." I shook my head

Goo raised his .45. "This what I mean about niggas in the hood, they never leave the hood. If you got out more you would have known, they gave you a paintball gun." Goo shook his head. "Take a walk with me, Zell."

Goo kept his gun aimed at me as he guided me under the Green Line train tracks on 39th right off State Street. I stopped walkin' when I saw Starks, Kira, Bubba, Jay, Baker, Big Curt, and Jake standin' around talkin' wit' guns in hand.

Goo leaned against the brick buildin' behind the tracks. As dark as it was, only a nosey mufucka would see what was happenin' back here. Now I knew that uneasy feelin' I had was death bein' near. Without a gun, I couldn't do shit but accept my fate.

Jay walked up to me and shot me once in the foot and once in the knee. I fell on the ground and screamed out in pain. "Ah shit!"

"How you gon' try to kill me? I used to be yo' brother. That hurt me, Zell." I could see the sarcasm all on his face when he talked. I took my eyes off Jay and followed the sound of something draggin' on the ground. I looked up to see Jake walkin' towards me draggin' a baseball bat. When he got close to me, he raised the bat up. Jake brought the bat down fast and hard on the same knee Jay shot me in. That made the pain a thousand times worse.

"Ah Shit!! I'mma kill you. I'mma kill all of y'all. Nigga I knew I should have killed you myself. This what I get for tryin' to put money in nigga's pockets. I'mma see you, Jay. Fuck!" The burnin' sensation from bein' shot was startin' to kick in. I wished I would have kept one of my pistols on me.

"What makes you so sure you getting out of here alive?" Baker asked steppin' closer to me wit' his gun pointed at my head.

"You pussy ass niggas can't kill me," I said even though I knew death was my only way out. Might as well go out like a man. "Ahhh!" I screamed when Jake whacked me in the stomach wit' the bat.

Baker laughed. "Coward ass nigga calling us pussies. You the same muthafucka that pulled that bitch ass move on Duke and had his own baby beat out of his girl. Not to mention fucked her friend, fucked his cousin's girl and shot her, stabbed Jay, and gave his new girl HIV before he mistakenly killed her. Not to mention you was a bitch ass snitch." Baker's bitch ass always was one step ahead of his competition. Too bad he didn't know about the letter I wrote that was gon' cause him some trouble because I knew he was gon' have Jay back when that shit hit the fan. I wonder how he knew about all that shit though. Fuck it. I'll never know now.

"I did all that shit and then some. The fuck you gon' do about it? And Cola knows that baby wasn't mine. Ask yo' cousin who baby that was," I laughed through all the pain my body was feelin'. Baker ain't one step ahead on this. I guarantee he was three steps behind when it came to Cola and Starks.

"Fuck you talking about?" Baker asked wit' a look of confusion. I smiled at the sudden uneasiness Starks displayed. He knew shit was about to hit the fan.

"You lookin' like you about to take a shit over there, Starks. You ain't tell yo' cousin you were fuckin' Cola. Fucked her in a car while it was light outside for anybody to see?" Starks looked at me givin' me a shut the fuck up look. "Ohm you ain't tell him? My bad, I thought he knew?"

Goo interrupted me. "Ain't nobody buying that bullshit you selling."

"Mufuckas was blowin' my phone up about that shit. I happened to be right around the corner from where they were at. I hopped in Boog truck, rode past and saw them. Cola's slut ass couldn't wait until y'all got to a bed. And don't think I didn't peep that shit at Boog's party that night. Fucked her in the bathroom while I was in the same buildin'. I still loved her lil slutty ass. I had that baby beat out of her because if it looked like him; I would have killed it." Baker looked at Starks readin' his guilty expression.

Baker took his eyes off me and looked at Starks. "Tell me somethin' Starks. Yo' silence saying a lot to me right. I don't wanna take what he saying and run wit' it."

"That happened a long time ago," Starks told Baker.

"Fuck you mean that happened a long time ago? You knew she was my girl when you met her. Why you ain't say shit then? One of y'all could have let me know somethin'." Baker kept his gun on me and his eyes on Starks as he talked. "Starks, you my family and you kept this shit from me."

"Serenity thought you would leave her if you found out about it. She asked me not to tell you."

"This shit better than a soap opera," I said as I watched the scene unfold.

"Best believe I'mma put a hole in yo' head if you say another word without bein' asked to," Bubba, the quiet one out the crew said.

"She asked you not to tell me. A'ight. What happened in that hotel?" Veins popped out of Baker's neck and head. I could see I hit a nerve wit' this shit here.

Starks spoke, "I wouldn't play you like that. You and her doing the family thing. I wouldn't be able to sleep at night if I did somethin' disloyal to you. I probably should have told you. I didn't feel the need to complicate y'all relationship wit' somethin' from the past." Even I could tell Starks was hidin' somethin'. He didn't really answer the question. He danced around the shit.

"Why I get the feeling you ain't telling me somethin'? Let me know if somethin' happened. Shit already bad wit' me and you right now. If I find out any extra shit, I don't know how I'mma handle that. Straight up."

"We blood Baker. It don't need to go that far over this."

"Right, fuck all that. What happened between you and her in that hotel?" Baker was mad, and I enjoyed every minute of it. Nigga gon' take my bitch and play house wit' her. Now he knew how I felt when I found out she was an ain't shit ass bitch.

Starks put his hand on his waist before he spoke. "We kissed. I stopped it before it got out of hand. She was acting off an assumption, and I had to be a man about the situation. I told her to put her clothes back on, and that was the end of it." When Starks said that I looked at Baker and saw how mad he was. I was goin' out wit' some mufuckin' entertainment. Me personally,

I would have used the shit to my advantage and blackmailed Cola's hoe ass. These mufuckas too loyal for me.

"Damn Starks," Jake said in the background.

"Starks that's some real fucked up shit. I took up for y'all ass when Baker was thinking somethin' went down wit' y'all in the hotel. You bogus as hell," Kira went off.

"Fuck you mean put her clothes back on? If y'all only kissed, she shouldn't have been naked. How the fuck that happen?" Baker yelled. One hand gripped a .44, and the other fist was balled up. I thought he was gon' go knock Starks out and pistolwhip him.

"I can't explain it Baker. Just know things didn't get out of hand." Starks kept his cool demeanor when he talked.

"Things did get out of hand if she was naked. So, who baby was it? Was it a possibility she was pregnant by you?"

"From what she say it was Zell's. He says otherwise. Only she knows the answer to that."

"Had I not had Tara 'nim beat Cola's ass, you just might be playin' step daddy to yo' own cousin right now. If you ask me I helped you out," I managed to laugh through all the pain I was feelin'.

Bow.

Baker shot me in my shoulder. "Shit! Ahh!"

"Shut the fuck up." He turned to Starks and shook his head, "If I can't trust my blood who can I trust?" Baker was in shock by what I told him. I was too when I saw Cola and Starks that day. That was the day I found out why Starks didn't mind followin' that bitch. Whole time I was thinkin' Cola was fuckin' Cash, it turned out to be Starks she was cheatin' on me wit'.

"Before I forget, tell Kee thanks for tellin' me about the barbecue. If it wasn't for her, I never would have found out about y'all plan. Tell her that I'm sorry I didn't kill you like she asked me to I guess my aim was off," I said between moans. My wounds were startin' to get to me.

"Kee ain't tell you shit," Jake said surely wit' a frown on his face.

"Check my phone," I said through shallow breaths. Goo came over to me, went in my pocket to get my phone, and gave it to Baker. The pain from bein' shot was startin' to get even worse. I started feelin' dizzy and weak. It was a struggle for me to breathe. I was fightin' to stay alert long enough to make sure they saw the messages from Kee.

Baker didn't look shocked when he read the texts from Kee. I guess he had enough shock for the night findin' out about his precious Cola and his loyal cousin. He showed Jay the messages then put my phone in his pocket. Kee probably would have told me about this if I wouldn't have pissed her off.

Damn, why I had to be so quick tempered all the time. I could have saved my own life and ended theirs if I had played my cards right. Thank God Anaya told me about her uncle and how close they were. I'mma haunt them from my grave through him and his niggas. I couldn't wait to see them in hell.

Baker, Jay, and Starks walked closer to me. Baker came the closest. He stood over me lookin' down on me wit' his .44 in his hand. Jay was in the background wit' Starks. They both had their guns in their hands.

Baker raised his .44 and aimed it at my head. "You can tell Kee yourself when you see her in the afterlife. She'll be there real soon. Tara really looked out for me. Running them blocks and telling me about everything you did. That was good shit." Before I could say anything, shots rang out.

Bow. Bow. Bow. Bow. Bow.

My body convulsed as I took five shots from Baker's gun. I was on my way to becomin' a memory. All of the people I crossed were standin' here while a nigga took my life. I guess what they said was true, what goes around comes around. I died lookin' my killer in his eyes.

Karma is a bitch.

Baker

Killin' Zell didn't go like I thought it would. I figured once I killed him me and Co could get back to normal. Instead, this nigga hit me wit' some straight up ether when he told me about her and Starks. Both of these muthafuckas had been looking me in the eye knowing they had a past. Walking around like they just met knowing they knew each other years ago. Couldn't neither one of them let me know what was up. Shit had me hot.

Without saying anything to anybody, I stepped over Zell's body and walked towards State Street where the cars were parked. My mind was fucked up behind all this shit. Maine and Trell sat in their car watching just in case Zell tried to run. Once I got in the car wit' them, Trell asked where I wanted to go. I told him to drop me off at the Hyatt on 22nd. I got a room wit' a view of downtown Chicago. The view took me back to when I was a lil one.

When I was younger I was always fascinated wit' the buildings downtown. My mama used to take me down there wit' her and I would ask her a million questions about the buildings. Who built it? How did they get it that tall without it falling? Why did they build it? Who told them they could build it? She thought I was gon' be an architect or somethin'.

She probably looking down on me disappointed that my life went in this direction. I think if she were still alive my life would be different. My mentality changed after my mama died. I didn't feel like I had nobody to make proud. My Aunt Carla stepped in and raised me, but she couldn't take the place of my mama. Nobody could replace her.

My phone vibrated in my pocket breaking me out of my thoughts. I looked at the screen and saw Cola's name and sent her to voicemail. Seeing her name made me mad all over again. Everybody was probably back at Big Curt's house by now.

She was probably wondering where I was and why I wasn't there. She started calling me back to back like she'd lost her mind. Every time she called, I ignored the call. I put my phone on silent and sat it on the nightstand next to the bed. I rolled up a blunt to smoke before I laid down.

In the middle of me smoking, I felt somethin' vibrate in my pocket. I forgot I had Zell's phone in my pocket until now. I looked at the screen to see Kee was calling. It took a lot for me not to answer the phone and go in on her snake ass. For now, I was gonna ignore her until I talked to Jay. We had to come up wit' a plan for Kee.

Early the next morning, I woke up to see sixty missed calls, fifty from Cola alone. I didn't bother to call her back. We were gon' be face to face soon. After I brushed my teeth and got myself together, I called Jay to come grab me from the hotel.

Jay pulled up a half an hour later. "What's up wit' it? Co out there going crazy. Talking about going to the police station to file a missing persons report. When she tried to go out looking for you, I let her know you knew about her and Starks. That shit crazy."

"Man bruh them keeping it from me is the problem. I can't be mad at shit that happened before me. They already know how I am about secrets and lying. I don't keep them, and I don't tell them. I'm a very understanding nigga." I shook my head.

"I feel you, Baker. Nigga tried to die wit' the upper hand until you flipped it on him and told him about his cousin. That fuck nigga had the nerve to look shocked. How about Kee tho? What's up wit' that shit?"

"Speaking of her snake ass. She hit Zell phone last night. We gotta dead her ass soon. I'm talking a couple days before word get out about Zell."

"I'm ready. I never would have thought Kee would pull some shit like this. She was a fraud just like Zell."

"I never would have thought yo' sister would pull some shit like the shit she pulled either."

"She kept it from me, too. I never knew shit about Starks. That caught me by surprise the same way it did you." I could sense that Jay knew more than what he was saying, but Cola was his sister. I didn't expect him to tell me shit about her. If I was in his shoes, I would stay out of it, too.

"Bruh I ain't trying to talk about this no longer. Me and Co about to do enough of that. What's the plan for Kee?"

For the rest of the ride to Big Curt's house, we talked about what Jay planned on doing to Kee. He wanted to take care of her, and that was cool wit' me. He had a nice plan, and we started putting it in motion as soon as he told me about it.

I sent Kee a text from Zell's phone pretending to be him saying I wanted to meet up wit' her to figure out the next move. She hit me right back and said she will be free on Sunday. I wasn't thrilled about waiting a couple days, but after asking if she was free later today, she just stopped responding to my texts.

Usually, I would be against killin' a woman, but Kee deserved it. Reading a text she sent Zell made me have a change of heart about killin' women. She told Zell to make sure he killed me when the opportunity presents itself at the barbecue. Kee even told him she would lure me outside if she had to. She earned a trip to meet her maker for setting that move up.

Walking in Big Curt's house, I spoke to everybody when I came in before I went to the bedroom Cola was in. She was in the bed knocked out. Looking at her laying there sleep was a sight for sore eyes. To this day she still was the most beautiful woman I'd seen in all my years. I understood why niggas came at her all the time. It was the same reason I did; she dope.

Wasn't no need to rush to have this type of talk. My words were still gon' be the same when she woke up. She needed rest for my lil ones anyway, so I let her sleep. I sat there thinking about the love I had for this woman. Cola was the second woman I've ever loved. I've cared about females in the past and loved one before her, but that love wasn't as deep as this.

We clicked from the moment we met. Instantly forming a friendship that led to a relationship. I never hid what I felt for her from her or nobody else. If I was gon' be ashamed to tell the world I love her, then I didn't need to be wit' her. Straight up.

It's fuckin' wit' me that she ain't let me know about her and Starks. Depending on what she said during our conversation, she was gon' make or break us. I hoped she said the right things. If she came clean I could forgive her about that hotel shit. It was gon' take some time and work, but it was possible.

Cola woke up an hour later wit' swollen, red eyes from crying. She sat up on the bed. "Baker I know you know about Starks and I. As much as I want to pretend that you don't, I can't. I wish I would have told you. It was before you. I didn't know he was your cousin." That was a bullshit excuse. I didn't wanna hear no bullshit right now.

"All that don't matter. You knew that muthafucka was my cousin when you met him. Why you ain't tell me then?"

"I was scared you wouldn't look at me the same. Losing you was the last thing I wanted to do. Starks didn't tell you because he saw how scared I was that you would leave me."

"I don't look at you the same because you kept some shit from me. You know more about me than anybody do. Cola, you supposed to be my other half, and you couldn't tell me about some bullshit that happened before you met me. For you to keep it a secret, meant it was deeper than just fuckin' to you."

Cola looked down at the floor to avoid eye contact wit' me. That move told it all. Once upon a time my girl and my cousin had feelings for each other. That was crazy as hell. Of all the niggas in the world, why she had to meet my cousin? And of all the women in the world, why did I have to cross her path? I wanted know, but I'll never know the answer to those questions.

"I'm sorry, Baker."

"What happened in the hotel?" Starks had already told me what happened. I wanted to know what she would tell me.

"Nothing happened, Baker." Cola was still looking at the floor. Jay must not have told her I knew everything. If he did, she wouldn't have lied to me.

I stood up and yelled, "What the fuck you lying for?!?! Starks already told me what the fuck happened! You steady trying me, Co. Most people in yo' shoes would come clean about everything. You pissing me the fuck off man. Straight up."

Cola let out a deep sigh, and I saw her tears hitting the hardwood floor. "I tried to have sex with Starks. He stopped me from making the biggest mistake I would have ever made in my life. I was mad at you. I wanted to do something I knew would make you mad. Having sex with Starks was the first thing that came to mind. I didn't think, Baker. I let my feelings dictate my actions. I'm so so sorry."

"So, who baby was it, Cola? Was it a possibility that you were pregnant by my cousin?" Truthfully, I didn't want the answer to this question. It was just best that I knew everything now, instead of dwelling on the shit after it was all said and done. Cola had a look on her face that told it all. She didn't have to say shit else. "Come on Cola damn! You was fuckin' the nigga raw! My cousin went in you bareback!" I blew air out of my mouth and shook my head. Hearing that made me not wanna look at her, let alone touch her. Yeah, that shit happened a long time ago, but it was the principle. Not only did she fuck Starks, she let him feel what it really felt like.

My eyes drifted from her face to between her legs. I stared between her legs for a few seconds. It didn't look the same to me. It no longer appealed to me. I used to couldn't wait to get in between her legs. Now, I didn't want it at all. If I had known from jump, it wouldn't have mattered. Them being secretive and shit made a big difference in how I was feeling and thinking.

Cola's sniffling and the sound of her cracked voice broke me out of my stare. "Baker, I really want us to get past this. I want our family to stay together."

"Yo' family just fell apart. Family can trust each other. I can't trust you. You should have been straight up wit' me. Instead, you was on some sneaky shit. I can't do it, Co."

"No! Baker we just got back together. Both of us were miserable not being together. Neither one of us can live without each other. Do you really wanna do this?" I couldn't stay wit' her feeling betrayed and left in the dark. I was a street nigga to the core, but that didn't mean I lacked emotion. I was a muthafuckin' man. Real men ain't ashamed to admit they have feelings. I was feeling fucked up right now.

"I really want you to do what's best for you because I'mma do what's best for me and leave you alone." I can't front; it killed me to say that to her. At the same time, I could only say what I felt, and that was what it was.

"We about to have three kids. I don't want them to be shuffled back and forth between your house and mine. How you gon' turn your back on us?" Cola put her hand on her small round belly as a way to make me feel bad. Low key, it worked. It didn't work well enough to make me change my mind.

"Don't try to pull that on me. You know damn well I ain't turning my back on y'all. I'mma still take care of you and my lil ones, but I ain't fuckin' wit' you like that." Same went for Starks.

If he got in some trouble, I would stand next to him in the line of fire. I'd walk wit' my blood to heaven or hell if need be. I just wasn't fuckin' wit' him on some kick it type shit though.

Cola's sadness turned into anger. She started yelling, "I'll take care of my kids on my own! I bet you won't see Londyn or the twins when they're born! Probably got another bitch you about to be with!"

"Using our kids as a way to hit me where it hurts ain't gon' work. One thing you ain't gon' do is keep my kids away from me. You should know that. I'mma let it slide because you hurt, and I know you not childish like that." Cola was starting to get under my skin. The best thing for the both of us was for me to walk away before I did or said somethin' I would later regret.

"Fuck you, Baker! Bald headed ass!" she screamed. I ignored her as I walked out of the room.

This breakup was even harder than the last. It wasn't just a lesson for a couple days like the other week. This might be permanent. I wasn't sure I could go back after this. I didn't lie or keep shit from her, I expected her to do the same. If I had a relationship wit' one of her friends before I met her, you better believe I would have told her about that shit immediately. She would then have the option to deal wit' me or leave me alone.

We held each other down for a nice lil minute without major problems until this shit. Co spazzed out like any other woman did. Nothing she did was ever enough to make me walk away from her for good. Loyalty and trust were two things I was big on. She made me question both of those things. If I had to question it that meant it wasn't there.

Co was my heart, and I was gonna miss her somethin' crazy. I just knew I was gon' see her walking down the aisle in that white dress It was crazy how things could change in the blink of an eye.

Cola

Eight Months Later

It had been eight months since Zell was killed. Sometimes I still couldn't believe he was behind every tragic thing that happened in my life. He deserved to die a slow death for everything he did to me and everybody else. Some of the stuff he did was just downright crazy. I was just happy he was a memory, and I could move on with my life.

Kee was nowhere to be found. Nobody had heard from her since she was texting Zell's phone after he was killed. Jay and Baker went to her old house and the hospital she was working at more than a few times looking for her. She moved out of the house and quit her job for some odd reason.

Jay tried his best every time they went to get her information from the receptionist, but she maintained her professionalism every time and never gave out Kee's information. They decided to give up on going to her job, but they never stopped looking for her. Jay even put money on her head. Nothing had come up yet. Kee was hiding out real good.

Light taps on the bathroom door broke my train of thought. I looked in the mirror and gave myself the once over before I opened the door. I couldn't believe I was about to go to the church for this wedding. My red hair hung past my shoulders in a bone straight wrap with a part in the middle. The long strapless white dress I had on fit my body like a glove. Having the twins changed my body completely. I was something like a vixen, and I loved it.

The taps on the door continued. I rushed to open it and gasped at the sight. "Oh, my God!! Londyn, what happened to your dress?"

"My juice did it, Mommy. B.J. made it fall out my mouth." The only thing I could do was laugh at the story she told on her baby brother who was only three months old. I grabbed her hand and pulled her in the bathroom. Londyn was standing there with red spots all over her white dress.

"Babygirl this dress was made just for today. You're the flower girl. Daddy might be mad if you don't have your dress on. He paid a lot of money for our dresses."

"But I'm Daddy's little lady," she smiled. Londyn still had Baker wrapped around her finger. She always will.

"I can't argue with that babygirl. We gon' put another dress on you after I go check on your brothers."

Londyn ran to her room while I went to the living room to check on B.J. and Zayden. They weren't identical twins, but they both looked every bit of their father even at their young age. It looked like Baker spit them out. I called them my little heart breakers. They had those same bluish gray eyes that Londyn and Baker had. Zayden was Baker's complexion, while B.J. developed my medium brown complexion.

I walked in the living room and saw a big red spot in the middle of the carpet. I could have killed Kira for sitting right here and letting the stain set in the light brown carpet. I don't know what kind of babysitter she was.

"Where were you when juice went all over the place? I thought you were babysitting while I got dressed," I asked Kira, who was bobbing her head to Yo Gotti's song Errrbody.

"On the phone arguing with Goo's ass. I need to be babysitting his ass. Then I got sidetracked when my boos wanted to lay their heads on my pillows," Kira laughed while holding both of my boys.

"You a damn pervert," I laughed. "I'm about to take my babies from you."

"Mommy, I got my dress on," Londyn twirled in her dress that was inside out and backwards. She was on her independent kick. She wanted to do everything herself. Londyn would bust a sweat before she gave up something she was trying to do. The dress she had on was her dress from her princess party a few months back. It was light pink instead of white like she was supposed to wear, but dressy enough for the wedding. Once I got her together, we'd be out of the door.

"Awww my mini me you look so pretty. I bet Mommy can make it look better." I picked Londyn up, sat her on the couch and put her dress on the right way. I fixed a few out of place hairs on her slick ponytail before I took B.J. out of Kira's arms and put him in his car seat so we could leave.

"Co, you look so pretty in that dress. If I was a nigga, I would hit that. Raw too," Kira laughed.

"You so damn silly," I laughed.

After I dressed B.J., we were out the door, heading to the church. When we walked through the doors, I started to get emotional. I wished my mother was here to see this day. She would be so proud to witness one of her kids getting married. I fought back the tears and carried Zayden and B.J. up the stairs in their car seats to where Jay and the rest of the men were.

I spoke to everybody then turned my attention on Jay. My baby brother was looking dapper in a black Armani suit. I took his appearance in from head to toe. When I looked down at his feet, I got pissed off. As nice as he looked, he had the nerve to have some all black Foamposites on his feet.

"Really Jay?" I pointed to his feet.

He looked down. "What? You muthafuc—. Oh shi—snap. I forgot where I was at for a minute. You people are lucky I got a suit on for this. I ain't a suit and tie type of nig—. Man I need to hurry up and get out of here."

I laughed. "Yes you do. Aside from the shoes you look nice, Jay."

"Thanks sis. You look decent."

"Decent. Boy please I look good." We both laughed.

Jay bent down to play with his nephews. "Zayden what's up homie? B.J. what's goin' on my man?" B.J. cracked a smile while Zayden looked at Jay like he was crazy. "Where the flower girl at?" Jay asked looking for Londyn.

"Over there with Marlene. She said the only person can see her is Baker. Is he here?"

"Where else that nigga gon' be, Co? He wouldn't miss this day," Goo spoke from the chair he was sitting in.

Jake turned and looked at Goo. "Nigga, how you gon' say nigga in the church?"

"The same way you just did. Plus God know my heart," Goo answered with a serious face. If I had some pearls, I would have clutched them listening to them.

I shook my head. "On that note, I need to leave them with you for a few minutes, Jay. Jake and Goo, don't corrupt my babies," I said as I walked towards the door.

Jake frowned. "I'm a saint."

"I'm just not gon' talk to them then, Cola," Goo said and everybody laughed.

On the other side of the church, all of us women were patiently waiting to get this show on the road. Everyone was giving me compliments on how I looked; it almost made me get a big head. We sat and talked amongst each other until it was time to start the wedding.

Marlene had the happiest smile on her face the whole time she stood face to face with the man she loved. Deep down, I was envious. Baker and I should have exchanged vows by now. Looking over at Baker standing as Jay's best man, I started having one of my sad moments about us not being together.

The feelings I had for that man would not leave for nothing. I needed to move on. There was no point of holding on to someone that didn't want me. I tried on a number of occasions to get Baker back, but he wasn't having it. What took the cake was when Kira told me he had another woman in his life. That cut me deep. It also made me realize it was really over with for us.

Jake and Goo cheering broke me out of my thoughts. My eyes left Baker and went back to the happy couple. Marlene was flashing her ring to the whole church after Jay put it on her finger. I was surprised to see her place a black diamond band on Jay's finger. The day he told me he was getting married I thought he was playing a joke on me. It wasn't until Marlene showed me her engagement ring that I believed it.

I wasn't trying to throw shade, but I saw a marriage full of problems. It was too soon for them to get married. Jay was not ready for this. Any man that wanted No Love by August Alsina to be his wedding song was not ready to be anybody's husband. Jay even had another female that he messed with from time to time.

I had to cover for him when Marlene called me looking for him. This other female didn't even know about Marlene. I hoped

Jay could get it together and leave the other girl alone before one or both of them fucked him up.

After the ceremony was over, Jay and Marlene got in his new black Benz and headed to my house in Country Club Hills where the reception was being held in the backyard. All of the guests smiled and waved to them as they pulled off. Kira decided to ride back with Goo after the wedding. She helped me get my kids to the silver Porsche Panamera Baker got me for Mother's Day last week.

"Co," Baker's voice came from behind me.

"What's, up Baker?" I asked while strapping Zayden in his car seat.

"You look nice today."

"Thanks, you too. White has always complimented you," I looked Baker up and down. He looked so good in his all white suit. After all these months of us not being together, he still made my heart melt and my love box throb at the sight of him.

"Thanks, Co," he smiled. "After the reception, can I take the kids for the weekend?"

"Is your little girlfriend gon' be around?" I asked with an attitude.

"You already said you don't want females around them. I respect that. I don't want another nigga around my kids. You know you ain't gotta worry about that. If I ain't wit' the female on some deep shit then she not gon' be around my lil ones."

"You can take them. Especially Zayden little mean self," I laughed. My little man kept a mean mug on his face. He was too little to always be looking mean. He wasn't gon' take no mess when he got older.

Baker laughed, "My son gon' be a no nonsense type of dude like his daddy."

"He just mean. I'll see you at the house. I know Londyn is tired of sitting in the car." I looked back at my car to see that the twins were sleeping and Londyn was playing with her tablet.

Baker leaned in my car and gave each of the kids a kiss before heading to his car. "Aight Co. I'll see you in a minute."

I pulled out of the parking lot feeling sad. I missed Baker, and I hated these conversations we had. We should still be living together not having conversations about him taking the kids for the weekend.

I checked my rearview mirror and Baker was right behind me in his white Porsche Panamera. I couldn't figure out why he'd gotten me the same car as him just a different color. I wasn't complaining; it just struck me as odd. Tears started to flood my eyes as I watched him smile while he talked on the phone.

I knew it was probably his little girlfriend. The smile he displayed was a smile of pleasure. The thought of another woman making him happy was still a lot for me to handle. Every now and then I shed a few tears over him. Today was one of those days. After eight months, I should be over him, but I wasn't. Baker always would be my everything.

I got myself together as I drove towards the expressway. Baker was still right behind me. I waited patiently for the light to turn green. When it did, I stepped on the gas and was hit by a red Honda that ran a red light. My car spun around and slid until a light pole stopped it from going any further.

Tires screeched right beside where my car was. I felt blood trickle down my forehead. Only two of my kids were crying, which had me on edge. Why wasn't Zayden crying? The stiffness of my neck wouldn't allow me to turn around to check on my babies. Their cries were becoming faint, and my eyes were getting low. Eventually, I didn't hear them crying at all.

Meechi

I stepped out of my cell to go on the yard to get some fresh air. I hadn't been out in almost a year thanks to a minor altercation I had with some lame ass nigga that came in trying to prove himself. I had to do a three in the hole. I couldn't get mail, make phone calls or leave my cell other than to take a shower. I was on the verge of going insane in there. I wouldn't wish the hole on my worst enemy. That shit would drive a crazy man crazy.

Once on the yard, I had to let my eyes adjust to the sunlight. When I finally could see clear, I started walking through the yard. I was greeted by all the guys that knew me and even some that didn't. That made me feel like I was back in the hood.

I got love from everybody just because my name used to ring bells in my project and every other project in Chicago. My reputation carried over in jail, and I got love from everybody in the joint. Shit, some of the guards used to be my customers.

Growing up in the Ickes, I had it all. Money, bitches, cars, and more bitches. I also had a woman named Saudia that I wouldn't let go of for nothing in the world. I kept her put up in a house out in South Holland. If we lived in the city, Saudia would find out about all my side bitches. I couldn't have that. She was liable to catch a murder charge for killing one of them bitches over me.

Since I'd been in the hole, I didn't know shit about shit on the outside or the inside. After I had talked to my homie, I was gonna call my girl to see what had been up. Her and my niece went ghost on me right before I went to the hole.

It's been over eight months since I'd heard from either of them. I told my girl I didn't want her to wait for me as long as she knew that shit stopped when I came home. She agreed and hadn't slacked up until a few months ago. I probably got a letter from her while I was in the hole. When I go back in, the guards should be passing out mail. As far as my niece, her hot ass probably laid up with a nigga.

I searched the yard for my big homie. I always showed him some love since I looked up to him when I was a shorty. I looked to my left and saw him leaning up against the fence that kept us all confined. Big Jay was a legend in the hood. All of us hardheaded young boys wanted to be like him, but only a few of us made it to the top. I was one of them. Unfortunately, following in his footsteps got me indicted. They gave me six years. I was lucky that was all I got. Some of the guys I was indicted with got hit with double-digit sentences.

"Big Jay, what's up?" I spoke when I got within earshot of him.

Big Jay turned to face me. "Look what the wind blew in. They finally let you outta that black hole. What's happening, Meechi?"

"Yeah, man. What's been up?"

"Not too much been going on inside of here. Same old shit just a different day," Big Jay said nonchalantly. He the only nigga I knew that acted like he didn't care about being locked up. He'd been in here for over twenty years and acted like it wasn't shit to him. Big Jay was a true gangster that bred a son that was a replica of him. I found it ironic that I wanted to be like Big Jay when I was coming up, and his son wanted to be like me during his absence. Getting to know Big Jay in here made me realize how much Jay was really like his father.

"What's the word on the outside? How Jay and Cola doing? She still with the same dude?" Big Jay looked at me with a screw face. He knew I had a lil thang for his daughter since way back when.

"They both good. Cola just had a set of twin boys and Jay got married today. The wedding probably just ended. I have to call them before we lock up for the night."

"Married?" That came as a shock to me. Jay had just as many bitches as I did when I was out. And he was a teenager back then. "Tell them both I said congratulations when you talk to them."

Big Jay nodded, "I'll pass the word."

We stood outside talking for the rest of the time we had left for yard. When the guards told us we had to go in, I went straight to the phone to try to call my girl. It was a long line for the phones since only two of them were working. Fuck it. I had to stand here I needed some money and a fuckin' visit from her ass.

After hearing a couple arguments and a little begging from the niggas using the phones before me, I finally got to a phone. The first time I called I got no answer. I hung up and tried again. Still no answer. Saudia had me ready to jump through this phone and choke slam her ass. I guess the third time was the charm.

"Hey baby! I miss you," she purred into the phone sexily.

"Fuck all that Saudia. Where the fuck you been? I don't wanna find out some nigga got you saying fuck me," I stated in a firm tone to let her know I meant what the fuck I said.

"Can't no nigga make me say fuck you. You my ten-year nigga."

"Yeah okay. I'm yo' ten-year nigga, but you been missing in action on me for a while. I been in the hole for eight months, and I bet you ain't sent a letter or shit." I got so mad thinking about what Saudia was out there doing I started sweating. I know niggas on the outside be coming at her left and right. She was a certified banger. Tall, light skinned, and thick as hell. She had long honey blonde hair that matched her hazel eyes and complexion perfectly. She had a small waist and an ass that went on for miles.

"I didn't write you. Sorry boo. I have been on the move doing something for my brother."

"You been with a nigga, Saudia? Go ahead and tell me."

"Yeah, I been with somebody else," she said that like it was normal or some shit.

"That's some bullshit! Cut that shit off today." I know I told her I didn't want her to wait for me, but that shit changed when she told me she'd been with another man. We had been together off and on for almost eleven years. I didn't want her with nobody besides me. I was about to come home. It was time to let dude's ass go.

"I can't cut it off with him right now." This bitch lucky I was not in her face. I would pop her right in that mouth of hers.

"What the fuck you mean you can't cut it off with him? When I come home I'mma show yo' ass something."

"You remember how that hot iron felt last time you tried to show me something?" Saudia was referring to the time I blacked her eye because some dude called her phone. This crazy bitch waited until I fell asleep and plugged an iron up.

When it got hot, she unplugged it and dropped the iron on my chest. She definitely left me with something to remember. I have a big ass iron print on my chest. After that, I never laid a hand on her again. I took the phone from my ear. I couldn't even say shit I just hung up.

I walked back to my cell still mad about the short conversation I had with Saudia. What kind of shit she on? Talking about some she can't cut dude off right now. I was foolin' when I came home. Saudia can bet on that. And if I find out this nigga still around when I come home, I'm killing her and him.

As soon as I stepped in my cell, the guard was coming through with the mail. When she called my name, she gave me a stack of letters. At least I knew I was thought about when I was in the hole. She had to hand me about twenty letters. I sat on my bunk and flipped through the letters. They were mostly from my grandma. The rest were from my other family members and my homie, Dan. I even had one from somebody that I didn't know. I'll read that one last.

I opened a random letter from my grandma first. Grandma Cookie always started her letter with a bible verse. I think I read the whole bible just from getting her letters. I had a smile on my face the whole time I read her words. When I got to the middle of the letter, that smile left my face. She mentioned that my sister was still tore up about my niece's death.

I didn't know my niece died. That came as a complete shock to me. I only had one niece. I took care of her like she was mine from the day she was born until I got locked up. We stayed close until she disappeared on me. That explained why she was ghost.

I went through the letters to search for one of the oldest letters from my granny. When I opened it, it didn't say nothing about my niece being dead. I wanted to know how she died. Was she sick and nobody told me? Was she in an accident? Did she get killed? I needed answers now.

I went through letter after letter until I found the one that explained what happened. I skipped the usual bible verse and any other words before I saw the words that popped out to me. My heart ached when I read that my niece was shot. I read on only to find out that the family found out she was HIV positive the day before she got killed. I couldn't process none of this shit. I took my hand and swept all the letters off my bunk. I ripped the letter that I just read up and watched the pieces fall to the floor.

My eyes were closed while my face was buried in my hands as I thought about my only niece, Anaya; my sister's only daughter. I remember going to my sister's house in Bellwood to put some money up or get some coke out of her basement since that's where I stashed everything, Anaya would run up to me and hug my leg when she was little. She would make me walk to the door with her little body wrapped around my leg. Her weak ass daddy didn't claim her, so I did his job for him. Anaya was like my fourth child.

The moment I opened my eyes I saw the letter from somebody named Zell. This was a name I didn't recognize. I picked the letter up and thought about the name on it trying to figure out if I heard it somewhere. The letter was light in weight. Whoever he was he must not have had much to say. Something was telling me to read it right now. I ripped it open and read the letter to myself.

Meechi,

You don't know me, and I don't know you. Yo' niece Anaya was my girl. From what she told me y'all was more like father and daughter rather than uncle and niece. I just wanted to let you know I got in touch wit' Dan and let him know exactly what happened to her. Get in touch with him A.S.A.P. That was some bullshit that happened to her. I miss my girl so much. I'm still mournin' her death. Make sure you get up wit' Dan...SOON.

Keep yo' head up,

Zell

No wonder I didn't know him. Anaya was always secretive about her boyfriends. She knew I would grill her about them. Fuck calling my grandma like I initially planned. I was about to call my nigga Dan right now. Something told me this Zell character told him something I wanted to hear. Shit didn't sound kosher either.

Baker

"Open yo' eyes, Co," I said as I noticed her eyes closing. I was right behind her when the car ran into her. That looked like some intentional shit. It was a couple of cars before hers. That Honda didn't move until Cola's car was in the middle of the intersection. Seeing that had me ready to go on a high-speed chase. Hearing Londyn screaming in Cola's car changed my thought process up.

"Daddy, wake Mommy up," Londyn whimpered. "Why won't Mommy talk to me?" she cried.

"Lil lady, Mommy gon' be okay. I promise. The people at the hospital gon' fix her." I hoped I wasn't lying to Londyn. Cola wasn't looking too good and that blood coming from her head definitely didn't look good. If her chest wasn't moving up and down, I would have thought she was dead.

"I wanna get out Daddy," Londyn cried.

"We gotta wait on the ambulance to get you out. They on the way." I didn't wanna move my kids just in case they had some broken bones or somethin'. The best thing for them to do for now was stay in the car.

Zayden was in his car seat with his eyes closed. The fact that he wasn't crying like B.J. told me somethin' was wrong. The only thing that let me know he was still alive was his lil chest moving up and down. The driver's side of the car took all of the damage.

Zayden felt the impact of the crash right along wit' Cola. My heart broke right then and there. Seeing my son in a dented car seat had me weak. I was mad as hell. I couldn't do nothing for him or Cola. That made me feel like shit.

I walked to the front of the car, leaned in the window, and felt Cola for a pulse. She had one, but it was faint. Seeing her bleeding and unconscious was fuckin' wit' me bad. I tried to talk to her to wake her up.

"Co, you need to wake up for me. Please wake up man. If not for me, for B.J., Londyn, and Zayden. Londyn will go crazy without you. Serenity, please get up man." When Cola didn't move, I felt numb. I didn't know what to do. We wasn't together, but I still loved her like crazy. I couldn't take her not being in my life in some kind of way.

Stepping back, I did the same thing to Zayden, "Zayden, you better be okay lil man. You know yo' mama would have a fit if she saw you like this. Come on Zayden let me know you hear me lil man. I love you, Zayden."

Staring at Zayden and Co almost brought me to tears. I thought about seeing him being born three months ago and holding him for the first time. Ain't no way my lil one gon' leave this earth today. Him or his mama. The more I stared at them, the more I was getting pissed the fuck off. A muthafucka purposely hit her car. That was some straight up bullshit.

The ambulance arrived within a few minutes. Once Londyn and B.J. were out of the car, I was leaning over the stretcher B.J. was on kissing him on the forehead. I looked up when I heard a paramedic scream for someone to grab Londyn. She broke away and ran towards me still crying and shook up. I picked her up and held her tightly. A paramedic came to check her out. She wanted to take Londyn to the hospital by ambulance, but Londyn wouldn't let me go. I wouldn't let her go either. I should have let her go to make sure she was good, but I couldn't put my lil lady down.

Cola was put on a stretcher wit' a neck brace on her neck. One paramedic was holding somethin' on her head to stop the bleeding as they rushed her to the ambulance. Her eyes were still closed when they put her in the ambulance. When Zayden was pulled out of the car, his eyes were open, and he was looking right up at the female paramedic. I ran up to him and kissed him wit' Londyn still glued to me.

"Where Mommy going?" Londyn asked wit' a scared look on her face and tears in her eyes.

"Mommy going to the hospital. We about to go see her now. Stop crying babygirl. You know I don't like when my lil lady cry," I kissed Londyn on her cheek to try to soothe her emotions.

I stepped on all the broken glass in the street to get Cola's purse out of her totaled car. After I got it, I ran to my car wit' Londyn still in my arms. She got in the back seat, and I sped off right behind the ambulance. Once I was somewhat calm, I called Jay.

"Bruh, Co was in a car accident. I'm on my way to the hospital now."

"What?!?!?!" Jay yelled. This supposed to be a muthafuckin happy day. I was just getting ready to do the Shmoney dance, now this. What the fuck man? Her and the kids cool?"

"Londyn wit' me. B.J. was okay. He went to the hospital wit' the paramedics. Zayden wasn't right when I first got to the car. When the paramedics got there, his eyes were open. Co been unconscious the whole time."

"Damn man. What hospital they taking them to?"

"Christ out in Oak Lawn. A muthafucka hit her car on purpose. I'mma holla at you when you get to the hospital."

"Man fuck that holla at me now. I'll come to the hospital after I kill whoever the fuck did that to her."

"Nah bruh, you need to see about her and yo' nephews right now. If everybody was cool in the car, I would have handled the shit right then and there. They more important right now."

"You right. I'm on my way."

"A'ight."

Twenty minutes later, we rushed through the hospital doors. I gave them Cola's ID and insurance card and any other information they needed on her and the twins. Me and my lil lady sat in the waiting room waiting for an update on the three of them. Londyn was in a chair next to me holding on to my arm that I had wrapped around her.

The doctor that was taking care of Zayden and B.J. came out about an hour after we got there and told us they would be fine. Other than some bumps and bruises on Zayden, he was good. My lil man was lucky. He took the impact of the car hitting a pole and only came out wit' a couple bruises. I was pissed that my lil ones had to go through some bullshit like this at such a young age, but thankful they were all good. Now all I needed was Co to be cool. I did somethin' I usually didn't do. I prayed.

Jay, Marlene, Kira, Jake and, Goo came running through the doors still wearing their suits and dresses. I was sitting there on edge because I'd been in this hospital for over an hour and hadn't seen Cola's doctor yet. Shit was making me wonder if she was gone, if she was in a coma or what. All I wanted to hear was her voice right now. I was also ready to murder the muthafucka that did this shit to her.

"What happened, Baker?" Goo asked as he picked Londyn up and sat her on his lap. I told everybody what happened, leaving out the part about this being done on purpose. Marlene wasn't as street savvy as Kira and the rest of the women in the crew. She was shook when Zell was her patient at the hospital. She would probably panic if I told everything.

"Why did this have to happen on our wedding day? Cola supposed to be at the house celebrating with us," Marlene said in a sad tone.

"We gon' celebrate when she come home. Cut all that sad stuff out girl. Cola gon' be good," he said while wrapping his arm around her.

"She better be good," Kira added. She grabbed Londyn from Goo, kissed her, and hugged her. I motioned for Jay, Jake, and Goo to walk to the vending machine wit' me. Once we were there, I put some money in it to get a juice and some chips for my lil lady.

"Now, who did this shit to her man?" Jay asked.

"Hold up," Goo said. "You saw who did it?"

"I didn't technically see who did it, but the shit blew my mind. Somebody hit her car on purpose. Muthafuckas tried to kill the reasons I live," I said through clenched teeth.

"What? Why? Zell in his grave and we don't got beef with nobody. Cola don't do nothing but take care of the kids. I know ain't nobody got beef with her. Why would somebody hit her car on purpose?" Goo asked. I wanted to know the same thing. If I didn't see the accident wit' my own eyes, I wouldn't believe it was intentional.

Jake frowned, "Yo' whoever it is bogus as hell for doing that shit wit' the kids in the car. They bogus for doing that shit period man."

"Damn can we just get money without all the extra shit? I know for a fact my sister don't have shit to do wit' whatever is going on. Whoever did that wants me or you Baker. They know Co is important to us and hurting her will hurt us."

"I already know Jay. We gotta figure out what's going on. I don't like having unknown enemies. A faceless enemy is the worst enemy to have." I looked at the faces of my guys and wished Starks was here. I had to fix shit wit' my cousin before it was too late. I'd been holding a grudge long enough. It felt like somethin' was missing wit' him not being around. If I could maintain a good relationship wit' Co, then I could do the same wit' Starks.

Everybody knew to stay on point when they were out. We did that anyway. Now we gotta be extra careful until we figured out what was going on. Jake told me he was gon' let his girl know what to listen for when she was in the hood. Goo already knew to pass the word to Kira. Big Curt and Bubba were down in Miami setting up a legit business to clean our money. Them my guys so I still had to let them know what was going on up here.

We turned around and walked back to where Kira, Marlene, and Londyn were. The twins' doctor was standing there, I assumed looking for me. He told me we could see them. We all went to the nursery to see them. Soon as we walked in the room I noticed Zayden had lil gash on the side of his head. Seeing that had me ready to go blow a nigga or bitch head off. B.J. was laying in his bed eating his hand up like he was starving. The nurse told me it was cool to pick him up and feed him. My lil dude went to town on his bottle. I'm happy my lil ones all good. My boys are some troopers. Straight up.

After I was done feeding B.J., I went back to the waiting room. My mind was all fucked up thinking about what just happened. If I have to tear this city up building by building to find whoever hit her car, I would do just that. While I was sitting here thinking my phone rang. I dug in my pocket for it and looked at the screen to see who it was. I sighed as I looked at the name that flashed across the screen. I didn't wanna talk right now, but I answered anyway.

"Yeah."

"Damn, why you answer the phone like that?" Saudia asked sounding disappointed that I didn't sound happy to talk to her.

Saudia was the woman I was dealing wit' right now. I met her at the car wash early one Saturday morning. We'd been fuckin' around for about four or five months. She was cool when she wasn't all in my ear bugging me about Co.

Saudia wasn't my girl, but I wasn't dealing wit' no other females at the moment. Having a lot of women was always unnecessary drama to me. I liked to stay drama free in that department. I just didn't want a relationship right now.

None of my people embraced Saudia. They were only down for Cola. Nobody mistreated Saudia, but they didn't try to get to know her either. She felt like an outsider around them. That made her not want to come around. That was a good thing though. Whenever we all did somethin' Cola or Jay was usually there. Ain't no telling how it would have gone if they bumped heads.

Part of the reason I wouldn't think about committing to Saudia or any other woman was because I still had feelings for Cola. At one point, I thought I was ready to move on from Co and let my feelings go. But thoughts of her were always somewhere in the back of my mind. I always wondered what she was doing or who she was wit'. According to Jay, she hadn't been with nobody else. The thought of Cola permanently not being around did somethin' to me today. I couldn't explain how it felt to see her like that.

"I ain't mean it like that. Cola and the kids was in a car accident. I'm at the hospital now."

"What hospital you at? I'm about to come be with you. Are the kids okay?"

"Stay where you at. My lil ones good though. Cola has been knocked out since the accident happened. I haven't heard anything about her."

"I'm happy the kids cool."

"Me too. I'm worried about Cola though. I kept talking to her, and she wouldn't get up. She can't leave these kids man. They need her. I need her to raise them wit' me."

"Boo you know I'll help you raise the kids if anything happens to her. I plan on being around for a long time."

I didn't get a chance to respond to the shit she just said because the doctor that saw Cola came out to talk to me. He told me Cola had a small concussion, but her brain activity was normal. She probably gon' have headaches for a few days and have to wear a neck brace for about a week due to the strain that was put on her neck when she hit her head. Within a day or two, she'd be ready to go home. I was glad she was cool. I didn't know if it was the prayer I said or if it just wasn't her time. Whatever it was I was thankful for it.

Cola was laying in the hospital bed wit' her back towards the door when I stepped inside her room. I pulled a chair up to her bed and rubbed my fingers through her hair. Not a lot of things got me emotional, but her and my kids always did it to me. When Zell violated her, I was mad as hell about that shit. When we broke up, I was hurt. I wasn't ashamed to admit that shit. Thinking her and Zayden was about to be gone forever had me damn near crying.

"Damn Co. I thought I was losing you forever. I'm glad you gon' be a'ight. Can't nobody do the job you do wit' our kids. When you get up I got some words for you about scaring me like that," I said to her not knowing if she could hear me or not. I just wanted to get that off my chest.

I sat there rubbing her head and thinking for a few hours. I had so much shit on my mind that I couldn't sort through the thoughts fast enough. Jay walked in the room and saw me kiss Cola on the forehead and smirked.

"I don't know why you keep acting like you ain't still pussy whipped over her. Y'all need to stop this bullshit and get back together. I heard don't nobody like that pie face ass girl you mess wit' anyway." Jay shook his head.

"It ain't that easy for me bruh. And how you know she got a pie face you never even met her."

"I don't wanna meet her. Fuck her. She ain't who you belong wit'." I knew Jay was right, but I wasn't gon' speak on this while Co was laying here like this.

"I hear you bruh."

Jay bust out singing, "Even when your hustlin' days are gone." He pointed to Cola, "She'll be by your side still holding on. Even when those twenties stop spending, and all those gold digging women disappear. She'll still be here."

"Yo' ass a straight up fool," I laughed. This nigga had tears coming down my eyes. I needed that laugh though.

"Let that shit go, Baker. Both of y'all still love each other. It wasn't like they was fuckin' behind yo' back. The world just ain't as big as we think it is. Co ain't had another nigga since y'all broke up. Once you hit that, y'all will be cool."

"Shut the hell up, Jay. And your singing is horrible," Cola said in a groggy voice.

"Damn ain't you supposed to be drugged up? Nosey ass," Jay said playfully as he sat on the bed next to Cola and gave her a hug.

"Baker, where my babies at?"

"They here, Co. How you feeling? You know what happened right?" I asked to make sure she was really good.

"Are my kids okay? How is Zayden? I didn't hear him crying in the car." Co was trying to get out the bed to go see Zayden. I loved the way she loved our kids. One thing I could never take away from her was how good of a mother she was.

"They all good sis. They over there chillin' wit' everybody." Jay made her stay in the bed. "I'mma go take a picture of them to show you." Jay got up and left the room.

"Cola, I'mma stay at yo' crib for a lil while to help you wit' the kids."

"Baker, you don't have to stay with me. I can handle them."

"You can't handle them while you in this condition. It's either that or I take them to my house and I know you not about to let that happen."

"You damn right I'm not."

Two days later, B.J., Zayden, and Cola were all released from the hospital. Cola was having a lot of headaches, and the pain medicine had her sleeping a lot. Most of my days was spent seeing after the kids. When they were sleep, I made calls to check on my money and everything else that was going on in the streets. When the kids woke up, I was back on daddy duty all over again. I couldn't front; I was loving this shit.

Saudia wasn't happy about me staying wit' Cola, but it wasn't nothing she could do about it. Co wasn't capable of taking care of the kids like she used to. I had to do what I had to do. If Saudia didn't like it then she could dismiss herself.

"Why couldn't you keep the kids at yo' house? Why you have to stay over there with her?" Saudia whined into the phone. I took the phone away from my ear. I didn't wanna hear her whining about this right now.

"Listen to me Saudia, my kids need their mama. If I had brought them to my house without her, Londyn would have had a fit. She already follows her around the house. Cola needs to have them around her anyway. It would be fucked up for me to separate them after what happened."

"So you just ain't consider how I would feel about this?" Here she go acting like she my girl. I shouldn't have given her my best sex. I should have kept that shit mediocre. Saudia ass be trippin'.

"Nah, I didn't think about that because it ain't about you right now. Only thing I'm worried about is my kids."

"Hmph, you ain't only worried about yo' kids."

"You think I'm over here fuckin' her? And you right I am worried about her. How can I not worry about the person my kids wake up to and depend on every day when they not wit' me? My only concern is making sure she okay. You trippin' hard as hell right now. I think you forget that we not together. To be honest, I'm doing a lil too much by explaining myself to you like we are. I'mma holla at you later," I hung up.

Saudia was starting to become a thorn in my side. We used to get along good as hell then shit took a turn for the worst recently. Every time I talked to her, she mentioned Cola's name. Last night, I met up wit' her for a few minutes, and she went so far as to ask me if she could come to Co's crib to meet her today. I think it's time I let her go.

"Uh, Oh. Sounds like trouble in love land," Cola said as she sat on the couch next to me.

I shook my head out of frustration. "I'm getting tired of her being in my ear about you."

"It's probably because I don't want her around the kids. The day you come to me and tell me you want to spend the rest of your life with her is the day she can be around them. Until then, she doesn't serve a purpose in their lives."

"Same goes for you. If a nigga ain't putting a ring on yo' finger then, he can't be nowhere near them."

If Cola were to tell me she was getting married, I would be mad as hell. A nigga stuck between a rock and a hard place. I loved Co and didn't wanna see her wit' nobody else. I was letting some shit from the past stop me from letting her know how I felt. The few women I'd been wit' after her just didn't do it for me.

I think me and Cola just needed to sit down and really talk about everything that went down between her and Starks. Maybe then I would know what I needed to do. Saudia making this so much easier for me wit' all her naggin'.

We sat in the living room and watched TV together. I told her I thought her car got hit on purpose. She agreed wit' me on that. Co couldn't believe somebody did that to her and neither could I. That was some wild shit to do to somebody. Not to mention wit' some kids in the car. The person that did it could have cost themselves their life trying to take Cola's. Whoever it was survived the crash, but they wouldn't survive me. Straight up.

Meechi

Ever since I'd gotten the letter from this Zell character, my mind had been all over the place. I still couldn't believe my niece was dead. It was eating me up that she'd gotten shot. If I were home, none of this would have happened to her.

I was sitting in the cafeteria looking at niggas devouring the slop they called food in here. Whoever was over the food program in jail needed to be an inmate right along with us. This shit had to be a controlled substance. All the people serving this slop should get a possession charge. I wasn't trying to eat steak or nothing, but the least they could do was serve shit that looked edible.

As soon as the guard said we could use the phone, I was the first one there. I hadn't been able to get in touch with Dan, and I wanted to know what Zell told him about Anaya. I dialed his number and waited for him to answer. I didn't get an answer. I was about to call again when the guard called me for a visit.

I walked to the visiting room wondering who was here to see me this early in the morning. When I stepped in the room, I saw Dan sitting down with his hands folded on top of the table. I looked at his appearance and couldn't believe how much weight he gained in a year. He had to be close to four hundred pounds.

He let himself go bad. Next to him was a female that I didn't recognize. She a cutie, but why was she here?

"I been waiting on you to call me man," he said when I sat down across from him. I'd been knowing Dan for fifteen years. We met through mutual friends in the hood and became partners in crime. Dan happened to be Saudia's brother.

"I had to do eight months in the hole. I just got outta there yesterday. What's the word? Who is this sitting next to you?" I didn't talk business in front of women. Most of them couldn't hold water. Dan knew better than to bring a woman with him to talk to me. She better have something important to say.

"Did you get a letter from some cat named Zell?"

"Yeah, I did. What's to that shit?" I asked curiously.

"He got up with me right before he sent you the letter. He told me he was there when the shit went down with Anaya. He gave me some names to check out. With the help of Jazzy," Dan tilted his head towards the girl before continuing, "I put faces to the names. One name I already knew. You know him very well. You locked up with his old man right now."

"I know it wasn't him?" I said in disbelief. Jay couldn't have been the one to kill Anaya. "What was his purpose?"

"Indeed he was. He had beef with Zell. Anaya got caught in the crossfire." I tried to process what I just heard. Jay killed my niece. That was crazy. Dan continued talking to me while I sat there. "Jazzy saw it and your grandma Cookie was there."

"How the fuck my grandma get there? She ain't know them. Did she see anything?" My mind was all over the place thinking about the shit Dan just told me. I really didn't wanna believe Jay killed my niece. It could have been anybody except for Jay.

"Your Grandma met them at the hospital when something happened to Cola. She became close with them. They invited her to the barbecue. That's all I really know as far as your grandma. I'll let Jazzy tell you what she know." Dan still had his hands folded on the table. He hadn't moved one time since I sat down. His seriousness let me know he believed what Zell told him, and he was ready to make a move.

I gave Jazzy a cold stare. "What you see shorty?" Part of me hoped she wasn't about to confirm that Jay was the triggerman. I molded that nigga into another me in the drug game. I would hate to have to give Dan the go ahead to put him in his grave.

Jazzy looked me in my eyes. "Well, first Cola and her girls jumped on Anaya and I don't know why. I was trying to break it up. They messed her up bad. After that happened, Zell was about to take her home. They bumped into Jay walking in the house while they were walking out. Zell and Jay had some words before Zell walked off. Then Jay and the rest of them went outside and started shooting at Zell. Anaya couldn't keep up with Zell and Jay shot her." Jazzy kept a straight face and never took her eyes off me. She was on the verge of tears telling me what happened to my niece. I wished I was free. I would go see Jay myself for this shit. He took somebody I loved from me now I'm about to take everybody he loved from him.

"How you know Dan?" I asked Jazzy wanting to know the nature of their relationship. "And how you know Jay shot her?"

"This my man," Jazzy said proudly while Dan smiled. It must be the money. She knew she didn't want his big ass. I wasn't tryna talk about my nigga or nothing, but if he didn't have money he wouldn't be able to get the caliber of women he got. "I know it was Jay because I saw him turn his gun towards Anaya while she was running."

"We met a little while after Zell reached out to me. We was pillow-talking one night, and everything about Jay and his crew came out. Saudia and her sister on top of something for me. Saudia sister was there and said the same thing Jazzy said about what happened to Anaya." So that was what Saudia been on. That bitch had always being difficult. She could have used a code to let me know she was on something. I wanted to know what Saudia and her sister was up to, but the guard came and stood on the wall right next to where we were sitting at.

"I'mma call my grandma after the visit is over with and talk to her about it." Dan gave me a look that let me know something else was on his mind. "What's up? Why you look like that?" I asked wanting to know what was on his mind.

"Man, your grandma sick. All of her organs are failing. She in the hospital right now. I went to see her yesterday. She couldn't even talk to me Meechi. The only thing she could do is grunt when I said something to her." That caught me off guard. I pretended like Dan didn't say anything about my grandma dying. Without my Grandma Cookie telling me what she knew, I had to trust what Dan was bringing to me.

Jazzy spoke up, "She didn't see nothing. She came out after everything was over with."

I looked at Dan and in a very low voice I said, "I want him and anybody that was shooting that day dead. I trust you to take care of this before I come home."

Dan cleared his throat, "I'm on it. You heard what I said about your grandma right?"

I stood up. "I heard you. Get in contact with my nephews, Steeno and Mark from out West. Tell them I said for them to help you with whatever. Keep Saudia safe while she doing what she doing."

I walked back to the dayroom like I didn't just get bad news. I don't want none of these niggas to be able to read me. On the inside, I was feeling fucked up about my niece and grandma. I wasn't even gon' ask the warden permission to go to the funeral. I wanted to remember her exactly the way she was when I last saw her, alive.

My eyes scanned the room for my Jamaican homie. I spotted him sitting in the middle of the room watching TV. I sat down at the table with him and watched TV until a commercial came on.

He turned to face me then asked what I needed and when. After I explained what I needed and how soon I needed it, he got up from the table and went to his cell.

Thirty minutes later, he came back to the dayroom and resumed watching TV. I sat there talking to the other guys for a while. My Jamaican homie finally told me to go check under his bunk for what I asked for. When I got it, I took it to my cell until I was ready to use it.

Hours had passed before Big Jay came out of his cell. Once I heard his voice; I went to my cell to get the shank my Jamaican homie made for me. I hid it in the sleeve of my shirt until I was ready to use it.

Big Jay was walking towards me. I secretly looked around to make sure the guards weren't doing their job. They never paid attention to shit until it was too late. That was gon' work to my advantage today. I also had to make sure Jay's best friend, Richie, wasn't in sight. He was on the other side of the day room gambling. I would be done before he knew what happened.

"What's happening, Meechi?" Big Jay said as he walked past me.

"What's up?"

When Big Jay took a few more steps, I got up with the shank in my hand. I crept up behind him in the crowded dayroom. I eased the shank out of my sleeve as I crept up on Big Jay. When I got close enough, I stabbed him in the back four times and slid the shank across the room to my Jamaican homie. Not only did he make the shanks, he got rid of them too.

When Big Jay fell, and people started to notice blood, I stepped away from him and pushed some white boy close to him. When the guards noticed what happened, they all had their weapons drawn yelling at us to lay on the floor. The white boy was looking like he was about to shit himself when the guards were yelling at him. I stayed on the ground watching Big Jay take shallow breaths and bleed all over the floor.

He did something that threw me off when the guards moved to let the nurse check him out. Big Jay looked at me and smiled. That meant he knew I did it. If he didn't die in the infirmary, I knew I was gonna have to watch my back. Big Jay gon' come for me, and he was gon' come hard if he lived.

Cola

"Co, you gon' come stay at my crib or go to a hotel?" Baker asked as he walked in the kitchen wearing a white tee and a pair of red basketball shorts. Ever since the accident, he'd been wanting me to come stay with him. He said if the person that hit my car knew about the wedding it was no telling what else they knew about. He wanted to keep me and the kids safe.

"Are you gon' take no for an answer?" I asked as I finished mixing the batter for the pancakes.

"Nah."

"You lucky," I said as I headed out of the kitchen.

"Why am I lucky?" he asked as he walked towards the stove

"You just are. Watch the food for me."

I left Baker in the kitchen while I went to check on the kids. B.J. and Londyn were in their rooms still asleep. When I peeked in on Zayden, he was in his crib looking around. When he saw my face, he got excited and started kicking his little legs. I smiled, picked him up, and gave him a million kisses while he tried to eat my face.

I was so glad my babies made it out of that accident alive. I didn't know what I would have done if one of them died. I was scared about the fact that someone tried to kill me, and we didn't know who or why. I thought after Zell died all the trouble would be over with. I just wanted to raise my kids and live my life in peace. I guess this was what I signed up for by falling in love with a drug dealer. In this lifestyle, sometimes people would get the people you love if they couldn't get to you. I think that's why my car got hit. I knew I wasn't the target. I barely left my house.

Zayden fell asleep minutes later. I put him back in his crib and went back downstairs. Baker was standing over the stove flipping the pancakes with his phone on speaker when I came back downstairs. I think he was having too much fun with those pancakes. I tried to take the spatula, and he held onto it for dear life. This fool almost elbowed me out of the way. I sat at the table listening to his conversation with Goo.

"Kira caught me getting my dick sucked last night," Goo explained.

"How the fuck she catch you? Where was you at?" Baker asked while flipping a pancake in the air. After he did it, he looked at me and winked. I laughed and finished listening as he talked to Goo about his night.

"In my car down the street from the house."

Baker laughed, "Goo you my mans, but that was some dumb shit. You could have gone anywhere, and you pick down the street from where you and Kira live. On top of that, you was outside."

"Home girl's man was in the house. She took care of me outside. The head was so good I didn't see Kira walk up. When she snatched the door open, shit got real. And you not about to believe what Kira did."

"I think I will believe it," Baker laughed. "What she do?"

"Kira put a knife to the back of the girl's neck and made her finish until I bust one. That was the most awkward nut I ever had. The shit felt good, but I couldn't react because Kira was looking at me the whole time. She probably would have killed me if she saw me react to the way it felt. It's real uncomfortable to get some head in front of yo' girl and a threesome ain't taking place." I burst out laughing then caught myself. I didn't want Goo to know I was listening. Baker had tears in his eyes from laughing so hard.

"Kira wild as hell. You lucky she ain't cut yo' dick off," Baker joked.

"I thought she was about to. She was looking at me holding the knife, and I was looking at her trying not to moan. That shit was crazy, Baker."

"All bullshit aside, Goo, you gotta be a lil more careful. You know somebody at us. You can't be out there like that."

"I know, Baker. I wasn't thinking about that."

Baker and Goo wrapped up their conversation about Kira and switched to business. He took his phone off speaker and handed me the spatula. Baker took his phone and went to another room to talk to Goo. I sat two plates out and started putting food on them. I'd heat Londyn's up when she woke up. I sat Baker's on the stove and sat at the table and thought about how much I missed cooking for him. I missed him so much it hurts. I would give anything to have him back in my life.

My phone vibrated against the table. I saw Kira's name and picked up. "Girl you crazy as hell."

Kira got right to it. "Goo won't be satisfied until I put his short ass in a pine box. Stupid ass left his phone on the bed while he took a shower. I looked in it and saw where he was about to go. I didn't meet him there; I beat him there. His stupid ass only went down the street. He was scared I was gon' chop his lil balls off."

"So what now? You and him on good terms?"

"Fuck him! I'm getting tired of this shit. One while he was doing so good, Co. I thought maybe he would keep it up. He fooled the fuck outta me. Not even a month after I was feeling all good about us, this happens. I love Goo, but he pushing me to my limit," Kira ranted. She knew she was not leaving Goo alone. I didn't know why she was complaining. They had a dysfunctional relationship, but it worked for them.

"Goo would be lost without you."

"Whateva', Co. He pissed me off last night and just now by letting his hype ass mama in here. I think she stole my panties last time she was here. Let somethin' come up missing this time. It's curtains for her ass."

I fell out laughing. "Kira, you lying."

"Girl no. They was new, too. Bitch probably sold my shit to get high. I would have went in Goo's stash and gave her some work if she would have asked. But anyway what's been going on? Baker been blowin' yo' back out over there." Kira laughed.

"Girl I wish. That's not the case at all." I really do wish that was the case. I missed the sex just as much as I missed him. I was mad this Saudia chick getting it. Even though I wanted to blame somebody else, I couldn't blame nobody for this breakup but myself.

"Rape that nigga then shit. He can't be walking around there not giving you the dick knowing you want it. If I were you, I would take it while he sleep. I do Goo like that all the time." Kira and I talked on the phone about nothing for the next few minutes. She was a hot mess. I was glad we'd grown closer over the past few months. She kept me laughing when we talked. It if wasn't a story about Goo, she was just being her normal crazy self. I loved Kira to pieces.

Later on that day, Baker left to go meet up with somebody. Before he left, he told me to have our bags packed and at the door because when he came back we were leaving my house. I didn't want him to leave me, but he told me he had somebody watching the house. I felt a little better knowing somebody was outside.

After I had packed our stuff, I took a pain pill because of the headache I was coming down with. I dozed off with the remote in my hand. I woke up a while later coughing violently. I opened my eyes and saw thick, black smoke coming under my door. I reached over and felt around for the flashlight I kept in my nightstand.

Cutting the flashlight on, I ran out my room with my shirt over my nose. I didn't care if I was running into the flames I wanted to get to my kids and get them out of the house. Londyn's room was right next to mine. Luckily, the smoke hadn't reached her room yet. She was in the bed knocked out. I put a shirt around her mouth and told her to hop on my back.

I rushed to Zayden's room after Londyn was on my back. His room was on the other side of the house. I prayed to God him and his brother would be okay by the time I got to them. I could hear the crackling of fire as I rushed to get to them. I kept calling out for Jay and Marlene. No one answered.

Zayden was in his crib sleep when I got to him. The smoke detectors started to go off, and I began to panic even more. I grabbed a blanket, draped it over Zayden and picked him up. I struggled hard with him and Londyn as we made our way to B.J.'s room through the smoke filled hallway. I hated myself for not putting them in the same room.

Londyn and I were coughing and struggling to breathe, but I was determined to get my son out of his room. Even if I died trying. I could hear sirens from a distance, but I didn't have time to wait. Londyn being on my back was starting to hurt my neck. I fought through that pain to get to my son. My kids were my world, and I would do whatever I had to do to protect them.

I was coughing so bad I thought I was gon' pass out before I got to my baby. B.J. was stirring in his crib, when I entered his room. I struggled to get him out of his crib with one arm. With a lot of effort, I got him out. I secured both of them in my arms under the blanket and rushed out of the room.

I was tripping over my own feet going down the stairs. I was in a hurry to get us out of this house. I wasn't sure if we would get out alive with me constantly tripping. I told Londyn to get down and hold on to me. The best chance we had to get out was if she walked. I could move faster with just B.J. and Zayden in my arms. Londyn held on to my shirt tight as we made our way down the rest of the stairs. I told them I loved them over and over through the coughs.

The three of them began to cry, and so did I. When I saw my living room in flames, I didn't know what to do. We had to pass the living room in order to get to either door. I looked around trying to see which door I could get to without putting my kids in any more danger than they were already in. The front door looked to be the safest.

"Londyn, you have to keep up with me okay. When I walk fast, you walk even faster."

"I want, Daddy," she sobbed.

"I want him, too."

I started to pick up my pace as we walked from the stairs to the door. I sighed from relief when I had my hand on the knob. Londyn screamed right next to me. I looked over at her and saw flames shoot up the arm of her pajama shirt.

Baker

When I pulled up to Saudia's block on 65th and Aberdeen it was like a typical summer day in the Chi. It was the end of May and the weather was already in the high 80's. Kids were scattered all over the place playing and being lil bad asses. The nosey people in the hood were on their porches watching everything and everybody. Niggas were outside standing by their cars trying to holla at any and every half naked female that walked by.

Saudia asked me to come over because she needed to talk to me. I wondered what she wanted to talk about the whole drive over here. I hope it wasn't about Co. She'd been trippin' too hard about Cola. I was sick of hearing that shit. Straight up.

The smell of Pine-Sol hit me as soon as she opened the door. I would never forget this smell. It smelled just my like my mama's house used to smell on Saturday mornings. My mama would be up before day sweeping and mopping wit' Pine-Sol. I wish I could smell this scent coming from my mama's house again.

"Hey boo," Saudia smiled seductively when she opened the door for me.

"What up doe?"

You got over here quick. I think you missed me," she winked.

"You think so?" I asked rhetorically before I walked to Saudia's bedroom to put my phone on her charger. Mine was completely dead. I took her phone off the charger and put mine on before I went back to the living room. "What up? What you wanna talk about?"

"I don't want us to keep arguing, Baker," Saudia said when we sat on the couch.

I looked Saudia in her hazel eyes. "That be you Saudia. If you think I'm not gon' make sure my kids looked after then I don't know what to tell you."

"Baker, I got jealous. I don't want you around the hoe you was about marry like this." I looked at Saudia. It wasn't no reason for her to call Co anything other than her name. "What?" Saudia shrugged. "That bitch is a hoe. She fucked yo' cous—" Saudia caught herself before she said too much. I never told her about Cola and Starks. I wondered who the fuck told her that. "My feelings are hurt Baker."

"That woman gave me three kids. I'm gon' be around her in some way sometimes regardless to what you want. Before this, I wasn't laying up at her house. I picked the kids up, gave her money, and called to check on them when I wasn't wit' them. That's all. Since I'm hurting yo' feelings or upsetting you by being a man then, we need to end this. I ain't trying to hurt you, Saudia."

Saudia looked at me like I was speaking a foreign language. It was time to cut this off anyway. I'd been fighting myself internally about my feelings for Co. I missed Co's ass man. I wanted to wake up next to her every morning and fall asleep next to her every night. I wanted see my kids everyday. I wanted my family all under one roof.

Saudia went to the bathroom and slammed the door. I didn't know she would take it this hard. It had to be done though. She expected me to not be around Co period and right now that was not happening. Our lil ones still young. If they were older and I was around Co the way I was now, I could understand the way Saudia felt. She was showing signs of a crazy woman and I wasn't wit' that.

I got up and went to the bathroom where Saudia was. I could hear her crying through the door. Pushing the door open, I saw her sitting on the edge of the tub wiping her face wit' her hands. I grabbed her arm, pulled her up, and gave her a hug. She held me tight while I rubbed her back. I personally thought it was too soon for her to be crying over me, but I couldn't fault her for feeling how she felt. Feelings were somethin' nobody could control.

I wiped her tears wit' some tissue and tossed it in the garbage can. I pushed her off me when I noticed a positive pregnancy test in the garbage. I looked at her stomach to see if she was showing any signs of being pregnant. Her stomach was still as flat as a board.

"What's that positive test I'm looking at in the garbage all about? I got three kids I know what them two lines mean. You Pregnant?" Saudia tried to leave out of the bathroom. When I grabbed her arm, she jerked away from me. Ain't this some shit. She was sitting here crying crocodile tears claiming she so hurt about me staying wit' Cola and it look like she been doing her the whole time.

"Mind yo' business," Saudia said while walking out of the bathroom. Her attitude changed real quick. She was just boohooing. Now she had some sass in her.

"A'ight just don't say that's mine. You know I don't fuck you without condoms and I flush them after I'm done. The one time it broke I took yo' ass right to Walgreens and made you take that Plan B pill in front of me. I bought a test for the last two months to make sure that shit worked. So if you thinking about it don't try to pull that one on me."

"It don't matter, Baker. You want yo' baby mama back. Go be with that bitch. If I'm pregnant, it ain't a matter you have to worry about," she said wit' an attitude.

"Only thing I gotta say is don't call me trying to start some bullshit. You and I both know," I pointed to her stomach, "That ain't mine."

"All the pussy and head I gave you and you still strung out over her. Pathetic ass, soft ass nigga." Saudia rolled her eyes.

"Pathetic? Since you wanna try me I'mma let you know a few things before I leave. If I was soft, that weak ass head you give and that second-rate pussy you got would have you driving that Porsche, not Cola. That raggedy ass Camry definitely wouldn't be sitting outside. You wouldn't have to ask me to pay a bill or two for you. I would pay all these bitches just because and hit you wit' bread to blow if I was a pathetic ass, soft ass nigga. You would have access to all my money, cars, and cribs. If I was soft you would have me."

Saudia just stood there wit' a dumb look on her face. She never saw me lose my cool before. She was saying whatever she wanted to thinking I was gon' keep my usual calm demeanor. I had to put her in her place before she said some shit that was gon' get her fucked up by Kira.

She yelled, "All you care about is that bitch and them ki—" I cut Saudia off before she said the wrong thing.

"Chill the fuck out and lower yo' voice. I know what you was about to say and I'm not gon' tolerate no muthafucka that got a problem wit' me giving a fuck about my kids' mama and my kids. If anything you should be glad to be fuckin' wit' me when all these kids out here got father's that don't give a fuck about them. You got life fucked up if you think you or any other woman gon' come between me and my lil ones. This shit between me and you is over wit'. If you got somethin' else you wanna say when I come back from getting my phone, we can address it. Think about it," I said as I walked away.

When I went to her bedroom to get my phone off the charger her phone was ringing. It was right next to mine and I saw the name and picture that was displayed on the screen. I wanted to dead her ass before I left. I decided against it for now.

I copied the number that was displayed on her phone into mine. She had a pair of ten-pound dumbbells laying in the middle of the floor. I took one of them and cracked her screen wit' it so she wouldn't be able to use her phone no time soon.

Saudia had the door already open for me when I came out of her room. She was standing there wit' her hands folded across her chest. I guess she ain't have shit else to say. It took all the gentleman in me not to knock the shit out of her when I past her. I shook my head and walked down the steps of her porch. I had a call and a stop to make before I went to get Co and my kids.

Saudia

I met Baker before all of the bullshit came about. We got along good as hell. I was probably on my way to becoming his main bitch when Dan told me what Zell told him. At first, I said I didn't want no parts of this because I was really feeling Baker. When Dan showed me the money, I was all for it. I couldn't turn down a nice chunk of change.

When I heard about Meechi's niece, Anaya getting killed. It bothered me big time. I was around that girl for ten years. She might as well been my niece. When Dan finally told me who did it, I immediately called my mother's other daughter, Kee. Since I knew those were her people, I figured she had to know what went down. My brother's girl, Jazzy confirmed what Kee said happened. I didn't really trust Jazzy because she just like me, was a paper chaser. I had my eye on her for my brother's sake. She had his fat ass nose wide open.

Kee had a vendetta against Cola and Jay ever since Cola put them paws on her. She fucked Kee up bad, and I didn't blame her for it. I would have beat her bloody too for fuckin' my man behind my back. New man or ex-man, Kee broke the girl code.

I repeated something Baker told me about Jay to Kee. She had a damn fit when I told her he was getting married. She wanted to know when and where. I thought she was just gon' crash the wedding, but this bitch looney bitch crashed her car into Cola's. I wonder where Kee was now. If I had a fuckin' phone, I could call her.

When Meechi gave Dan the head nod, we linked up with Kee and came up with a few ideas on how to go about things. Somewhere in between Baker dickin' me down proper and him just being a nice guy, a bitch caught feelings and developed a conscience. I started playing the jealous role to push Baker away from me. Lord knows I couldn't walk away from his fine ass on my own. Besides that, Dan and Meechi would never let me be with Baker without trying to kill him.

I had been sitting here trying to think of a lie to tell my brother about why Baker left before he got a chance to come over. Dan was coming to kill Baker. I couldn't let it go down on my watch. If Baker was any other nigga, I wouldn't give a quick fuck about him. It was something about him that wouldn't allow me to let him get hurt if I could help it.

The sound of my door creaking scared me a little bit. I saw Dan creeping inside with a Mac 11 in hand. He looked at me sitting on my windowpane, and I shook my head.

"Where he at?"

"Big bro he left. He said he wasn't rockin' with me nomo'. I would have called you, but my phone mysteriously broke," I lied. I knew Baker broke my phone before he left. But for what?

"Damn, Saudia. You couldn't keep him here?"

"Nope."

"We just gonna have to hit the streets then."

"Yeah, you do that," I said letting Dan know I wasn't about to be in the streets with him. Being in the streets meant guns blazing. Saudia wasn't for the gunplay. "Where Kee at? You heard from her today?"

"That's your sister not mine. Why would I hear from her?" Dan said in a smart tone. Dan and me shared the same father while me and Kee shared the same mother. Kee was conceived during a rape, and out mother hated her. I had an unexpected encounter with her at the hospital she worked at, and that was how we got in touch.

"Cause y'all got something in common right now. Y'all need to talk and coordinate plans."

"Hold up. What you mean y'all? You not in it with us? Or you in love with Baker?" Dan squinted his eyes and looked at me searching for an answer.

"Nigga, please. I love Meechi!" I screamed. I did love my nigga, but he couldn't do shit for me from where he at. I'd been doing me since he'd been gone. I wouldn't let Dan know that though. His fat ass would probably tell Meechi. Sometimes I wondered who he was related to. He looked out for Meechi more than he did for me at times.

"Yeah Okay, Saudi Audi." I hated when Dan called me that shit. He only called me that when I said something he didn't believe.

"Did Kee do that today?" Kee was supposed to do some crazy shit today. I hope she knew what she would be in for if this didn't go as planned and they found out it was her. I thought I was crazy, but Kee took the fuckin' cake. The shit she was supposed to do was another reason why I had Baker come to me. Fuck his baby mama. I only wanted to protect him.

"She said she was gonna wait until it got dark outside to do it." Dan said before answered his ringing phone. "Steeno, what's up?...You looking at him right now?...He don't see you watching?...Surprise him," Dan said before he hung up.

As soon as Dan said the word surprise, I knew whoever Steeno was looking at was about to be dead. Even though Baker just treated me and told me I had some second-rate pussy and weak head, I hoped it wasn't him. I provoked him to say everything he said to me. He was a damn lie anyway, so I wasn't mad at him.

I looked at my stomach and thought about the decision I had to make before Meechi came home. I purposely went in the bathroom knowing Baker would see the test and leave me alone for real for real. My little secret of the last few years popped me off, and I didn't know what to do about it. I wasn't equipped to be nobody's mama. Shit, I wasn't playing with a full deck; I knew this baby would be extra fucked up. Decisions, Decisions.

Baker

"What up doe cuz?" I said when Starks picked up the phone as I pulled away from Saudia's house. Me and Starks hadn't spoken a word to each other since Zell told me about him and Co. That was about to change today. If I knew my cousin, he was gon' act like we never stopped talking.

"On Western looking at some used cars for the winter." Starks was really looking at cars to make drop-offs in. That was the code we used just in case anybody was listening. "What's up?"

"Aye we gotta put the past in the past before it's too late. Shit getting real again, and it made me realize how short life is. I should have been let shit go."

"Say no more, Baker. No matter what happens between us, or how long we go without talking, our veins still got the same blood running through them. What's going on? I know it ain't nobody causing you problems."

"A muthafucka hit Co car not too long ago. I just left Saudia's crib and saw Kee calling her phone. You already know I'm on top of that. I need to find out how they connected and where Kee's at. I'm on my way to Jake's girl crib, so she can call Kee and pretend to be Saudia."

"Let me know what you need from me. I got yo' back cuz," Starks said eager to lend a helping hand wit' whatever I needed.

"Be ready."

"Come on, Baker, you know I stay ready, so I don't have to get ready. I'mma hit you in the a.m."

"A'ight," I hung up. It felt good to talk to Starks after all this time. He was the missing piece to the puzzle. Shit was gon' feel right again now that Starks was gon' be back around.

A blunt and my nigga Jeezy would keep me company on the way from the South side to the West side. Jeezy had all the hood classics. No matter how old his shit was, I would listen to it like it just came out. I was on his new shit, Seen It All right now. His song, 4 Zones was blasting through my speakers as I rode out West.

When I pulled up in front of the house on Homan and Ohio, I noticed a group of guys standing on the porch. I made sure I had my .45 on me before I got out of the car. I knew these niggas, but not like I knew my niggas. Just because I spoke to them didn't mean they wouldn't try me. After I put the blunt out, I took the keys out the ignition and got out the car.

"What up doe?" I said to everybody on the porch.

"What's good, Baker? Can I talk to you when you done in there? It's important," A young boy named Q asked me.

"Give me about ten, fifteen minutes."

I opened the screen door and walked inside the house. The smell of Kush hit me instantly making me higher than I already was. I sat on the couch, pulled five hundred dollar bills out of my pocket, and put them on the table.

"Do me a favor Xotica."

"Nigga hi to you, too," Xotica said as she blew smoke in my direction. Xotica was Jake's girl. She cool people and just what Jake liked. A bad chick wit' a lot of attitude. Her and Kira think they long lost sisters because they acted just alike. The only thing I didn't like about Xotica was that she kept a lot of traffic in and out of her house. Niggas stayed on the porch wit' her lil brother Q and females stayed coming in and out kicking it wit' her.

"My bad. What up doe?"

"Naw, nigga don't speak now. What you want?" I gave Xotica instructions on what I needed her to do. She was down for it. I love my niggas and their girls. We all knew the meaning of loyalty. The only thing can break me, and my people is death. "Get that money off my table. You my people. I ain't gon' take that from you."

"Girl you better take that cash. You got bills to pay in here," Jake said as he came through the door holding two duffle bags.

"Naw bitch I don't. You gon' pay these bills in here," Xotica snapped. I laughed because in the year that they'd been together, I never heard her call Jake by his name. To her his name was bitch. Next to Kira and Goo they were the funniest couple I had ever met.

"What up doe?" I said as Jake stood at the table and dumped the money out of the duffle bag.

"Trying not to catch a domestic. What's up fool?"

"Try me!" Xotica shouted.

"Chill, Xotica. Get ready to make this call for me."

"Nigga, I'm ready. Is you ready?"

"Now I'm about to catch an assault and battery on yo' ass," I joked.

"Try me, Baker!" Xotica laughed.

Xotica said a few words to Jake before walking to the bedroom. I told Jake to make sure the front door was locked, and nobody came in. He told Q not to let nobody knock on the door and don't come in for a few minutes.

Xotica sat on the bed, and I leaned on the doorframe. Before Xotica made the call, my phone rang. It was my Aunt Carla. I sent her to voicemail. I needed to find out about Kee and Saudia. I didn't get a chance to put my phone in my pocket before she called me back. I figured it was important, so I answered the call.

"What up doe?...Huh? Calm down and talk to me...What?!?!...Starks dead! I just talked to him twenty minutes ago!...I'm on my way to yo' crib," I hung up the phone.

Jake rushed to the room where I was and asked me what happened. I told him what happened to Starks, and he told me he was about to ride wit' me to my Aunt Carla's crib. I told Xotica to still make the call and hit me when she found somethin' out.

I rushed out the room wit' my phone to my ear trying to get in touch wit' Goo to tell him about Starks. Jake rushed out right behind me tucking a .44 in his waist. Q and his guys were still on the porch when I opened the door. He was ready to talk, but I didn't have time. I told him to get my number from Jake and hit my phone at a later date. We hopped in my Range, and I peeled off like I was being chased.

I was doing at least eighty to get to my auntie's house out in Richton Park. It just fucked me completely up to hear Starks was dead. I just got back in tune wit' him today. That was what make the shit so crazy. I just heard his voice now he was gone. I wasted valuable time holding on to some bullshit instead of kicking it wit' my cousin. Starks never even met my boys. Damn man. I feel fucked up.

I pulled up to my auntie house not giving a fuck how I parked my car. I damn near scraped my shit on the curb. I didn't give a fuck. All I wanted to do was find out about Starks. Jake and me hopped out the car quickly and sprinted up to the door.

I banged on her door like the police. I could hear my auntie screaming and crying through the door. My uncle B opened the door, and I could see the pain in his eyes from losing his only son. He had tears welled up in his eyes, and it killed me to look at him.

I walked over to my Aunt Carla, who was on her knees in the middle of the floor balling out of control. I pulled her up and gave her a hug. I held her in the middle of the floor until she stopped crying. She kept asking me why. I couldn't answer that question. I wanted the answer to that myself.

After a couple hours, my auntie got herself together. B put her in the bed to lay down and get some rest. Once he came back out, we all stepped on the porch to get some fresh air. We stood there not saying a word to each other. The air felt different, and the sun wasn't shining as bright as it was before. It didn't feel right already without Starks being alive.

"B, what happened to him?" Jake asked. B didn't look at us. He just stared into space and started talking.

"He went to look at some cars. He didn't see nothing he liked at the first car lot. He called me, and I told him to go on 66th and Western to a friend of mine lot," B choked up a lil. "From the story I got. Starks was sitting inside one of the cars checking it out when somebody came from behind another car and shot him in the head," B said as he let his tears roll down his face.

"Yo' people got a security system unc?" I would go pay to get those tapes before the police do.

"Nephew, I already thought what you thinking. Only one of his cameras work. The camera was on a completely different angle from where Starks was killed. I got there and saw my son in that car with his eyes open and a hole in his head." B just let the tears keep falling. I guess that old Scarface song was true because I'd never seen a man cry until I saw a man die. "I've seen death a lot, but this is the first and only time it had an effect on me." B turned to me, "Make sure you not next nephew." That was a warning from B for me to be careful.

It was dark out when me and Jake headed back West. While driving Goo called me back, and I broke the news to him about Starks. Me, Jake, and Goo had known each other for over ten years. It ate all of us up to have to bury Starks. I wasn't ready to put my cousin in the dirt. He was the true definition of a day one nigga.

When we got back to Jake's girl crib, she was sitting on the porch smoking a cigarette. She looked like she was pissed about somethin'. Jake got out the car and walked over to her. I was about to pull off when Jake called my name. Him and Xotica walked over to my car and got in.

"What up?" I asked no one in particular.

"Baker pull off and drive to Cola's house," I did what Xotica said wondering why they were coming wit' me.

"What up y'all?"

"I called Kee like you asked me to. I recorded the conversation because I didn't wanna miss nothing. I'm about to play it for you. Xotica passed Jake her phone in the passenger's seat, so I could hear the conversation clear. Jake played the recording, and I listened as I drove.

"Hello?"

"Hey girl. This Saudia," Xotica said when she got an answer.

"Hey Pooh. Who number is this? And why you sound like that?" Kee asked.

"This my new number. I'm doing my hair. I got you on speaker."Xotica lied.

"Oh okay. I set Cola house on fire tonight."

"You did what?!?! Bitch how you find her house?" Xotica asked shocked.

"Why you acting all surprised like you didn't know what I was about to do? Pooh stop playing dumb. That night Baker met you after I hit Cola car I came to where y'all was at and followed him back to her house. Since your brother knew what kind of car Jay drives, and I spotted it in front of her house, I took it upon myself to kill two birds wit' one stone. I told them I would be back. Now I need my money from your brother."

"I'll call him and tell him you came through." Xotica played along not knowing what was going on. "Where you at now?"

"At the Amber Inn on 39th and Michigan."

"Okay. Well let me finish doing my hair. Talk to you later."

"Okay sis."

"That's the end of it, Baker. I swear on my life if you need me for anything I'm down. These goofy ass bitches got me heated," Xotica said as she lit up another cigarette.

So these bitches are sisters and Saudia got a brother. Kee hit Co's car, and she said she set the house on fire. I started calling Co back-to-back trying to get an answer. Her and my lil ones faces popped in my head when she didn't answer.

The vein in my neck popped out, and I stepped on the gas. These muthafuckas just dug their own graves. Shit was about to get real now. Saudia and Kee got some loose screws, and I was gon' tighten them bitches up. I got somethin' in store for Saudia that she would always remember me for. I stopped myself when I was about to dial Starks' number. He was always ready for whatever. I was fucked up knowing he wouldn't be standing on the frontlines wit' me.

I dialed Cola's number once again. She still didn't answer. I hoped she was sleep or somethin'. If I got here and I saw anything on fire muthafuckas better get ready to die. They all just fucked themselves wit' no lube by coming for mine. I'll bet my last dollar Saudia's brother had a hand in Starks getting killed.

As soon as I got close to Cola's house I could smell smoke. These people better be out here having a barbecue or somethin'. Jake was on the phone sending some of our young boys to watch the hotel for Kee. Xotica had a worried look on her face when the scent hit her nose.

I tried to make the turn on Cola's block, but couldn't get through because the police had the street blocked off. From where I was, I couldn't see nothing but flashing blue and red lights. I drove to the next block and parked my car in the first space I saw. I ran over to Cola's block and froze in place when I saw her house engulfed in flames.

Cola

"Help!! Oh my God!! Oh my God!! Oh my God!! Help my baby! Please!" I screamed as Londyn cried and screamed out in pain through coughs. Some of the firemen rushed to me and the twins to move us out of the way. The other's saved Londyn's life. The fire on her arm was out, but she was still screaming and crying from the pain it caused. I wished I could take her place and feel that pain she was feeling.

The twins were crying, and Londyn's arm was burned and I was just, I don't know what I was right now. All four of us needed oxygen masks. Tears fell down my cheeks as I looked at my daughter's arm. I felt like I failed her. As her parent, I was supposed to protect her, and I didn't. She got burned because I told her we could move faster if she got down. This was my fault, and I would never forgive myself for it.

I heard Baker's voice yelling my name from a distance. My mind was so gone I didn't even respond to his calls. Londyn was put in the back of an ambulance, and I refused to let her go to the hospital alone. The paramedics wouldn't allow all four of us to ride since we all needed some type of treatment. Smoke inhalation or not I wasn't leaving Londyn's side.

Baker came up behind me, took one look at Londyn and turned beet red. He was so mad the veins in his neck and forehead popped out so much I thought they would pop. I told him to ride in the ambulance with the twins, and I would ride with Londyn. They wanted the twins to go in separate ambulances, but Baker went off, and they let them ride together.

The ambulance took us to South Suburban Hospital. I cried the whole way there. I prayed to God that Londyn would forgive me for what happened to her. As soon as we got to the hospital Londyn and the twins were taken to the back. I didn't want treatment; I wanted to be right there when the Doctors came out with any news on my kids. The lingering cough I had was nothing compared to my daughter getting burned.

Baker sat next to me in the waiting room without saying a word. He was still red, and the veins in his neck and head were still visible. I looked at him and let out a loud cry. He held me in his arms and let me cry it out.

"Why does stuff keep happening to my kids? First Zayden; now Londyn. I can't take it Baker. I can't take it," I sobbed as I cried on his shoulder.

"Tell me what happened in the house, Co," Baker said as he rubbed my back. I told Baker what happened. I still don't understand how my house caught fire. "How did Londyn get burned?"

"I don't know Baker. I was focused on getting us out of there. When I looked back the shirt that I gave her to cover her mouth was laying on the floor burning, and she was screaming because her pajama shirt caught fire. I hope she forgives me Baker."

"Look at me," Baker said as he held me. I raised my head and looked him in his eyes. "This ain't yo' fault. You did good. Think about all the parents that would have left the kids in the house to save themselves. Or got one child, but left before they could get the others. You got all three of our lil ones outta there. Londyn might have gotten burned, but it could have been worse. She not gon' hate you for her getting hurt. She gon' love you for saving her."

"But I didn't protect her," I cried.

"Yes you did. She was in her room still sleep. She could have died. You did more than protect her. You saved her," Baker kissed me on the cheek. "I couldn't ask for a better mother for my kids. Straight up."

Londyn's doctor came out of her room an hour later. She told us Londyn had second-degree burns on her hand and lower arm. The good news was that her burns were superficial. The doctor said she would heal in a couple of weeks with minimal scarring. Most of Londyn's treatment would be at home. All she needed was pain medication when needed and the gauze on her arm to be changed three times a day after we cleaned and put ointment on her.

A couple of uniformed officers approached us in the waiting room. They had questions about the fire. They said they suspected arson. They had to wait on the fire department to do an investigation before they could confirm it. It couldn't have been arson. Who would do something like that?

My babies had to stay the night in the hospital, so Baker and I went in the Parent room. It had reclining chairs, a couch, a full bathroom, a TV, a microwave, and a fridge. My clothes smelled like smoke, and I wanted to take a shower. Baker managed to get me a jogging suit to change into from somewhere. I washed my hair in the shower and pulled it into a ponytail. Baker was on the phone when I sat in one of the recliners directly across from him. He looked at me and got off the phone.

"You a'ight?" he asked while putting his phone in his pocket.

"I'm fine. Are you okay?"

"I'm good. Why you all the way over there? Come sit next to me."

I walked over to Baker and sat next to him. He pulled me close to him and kissed my forehead. "What them people talking about?"

"They think somebody set the house on fire."

Baker took a deep breath, "Somebody did set it on fire."

I pulled away from Baker. "What? How you know?" Baker told me how he found out Kee set my house on fire. Kee hurt two of my kids already. She not gon' get the chance to hurt them again. I used to let this bitch babysit Londyn when Baker and I wanted some time for ourselves. I was ready to kill Kee before.

Now her and Saudia was on my shit list. They better hope I didn't come across them no time soon. You had to be a sick person to do shit like this to kids. They worse than Zell was. Crazy bitches.

"Baker, I'm killing both of them unstable bitches for this shit. Where that bitch Saudia live at?"

"Co, I got somethin' else in mind for Saudia. Let me take care of everything."

"I still wanna whoop her ass. Her ass, Kee's ass and whoever her brother is ass." I was steaming. Fuck what Baker talking about. If I find either of them, Baker better get ready to take care of the kids because I'm going to jail for murder.

"When Xotica was playing like she was Saudia earlier Kee kept calling her Pooh. You know anything about that?"

"Are you fuckin' serious?" Baker nodded. "Pooh is Kee's sister name. Saudia is Pooh? Oh my God." I was in complete disbelief that Kee and Saudia were related. I never knew Saudia, Pooh or whatever the fuck you wanna call her when Kee and I were growing up. Kee was never allowed to have company back then. I never stepped foot in her house. Her mother really despised her.

"Straight up? I'mma handle it. I'm a humble nigga, but I don't tolerate nobody causing my kids harm. I don't give a fuck who it is." Baker was pissed off and so was I. These two bitches were playing with my life and my kids' lives. Baker would go to war against a million people for our kids and I would too. Kee should know better.

"So did you just happen to meet Saudia?" I asked curiously.

"I don't know. I plan on finding all that out when the kids get outta here and I get you settled at my house. I'm sure it was her brother." When I looked at Baker, I could tell something else was bothering him. I know him like the back of my hand. It was something else going on in that mind of his.

"Baker, what else is on your mind?" I asked wanting to comfort him the same way he comforted me.

"Just had a bad day, Co."

"What happened?"

Baker took a deep breath, "Starks got killed today."

"What?!?!" I yelled in shock. "Why didn't you tell me this when you got here?"

"Because he gone and you and my kids not. He wouldn't want me worried about him while my kids in here."

"What happened to him, Baker?"

"He got shot at a car lot," Baker said with sadness in his eyes.

"I'm so sorry, Baker. You know I'm here if you need me."

"I know, Co, I appreciate you."

Baker gave me the details of Starks' death, and I wanted to cry for him. I hated to hear that Starks was dead. I felt for Baker and his aunt and uncle. I really felt for Baker when he told me he talked to Starks for the first time today since finding out about our history together. They talked right before he died.

I could only imagine how he felt inside. Baker said he didn't want to talk about it anymore and he wanted to focus on the kids. I agreed not to bring Starks' death up unless he did. I fell asleep with my head resting on his shoulder.

Baker was on the phone with Kira going over what they had planned for Saudia when I woke up in the middle of the night to go look in on our kids. The twins were in the nursery sleeping and Londyn was in her room sleep. I went back to the Parent room and turned on the TV.

I saw what was left of my house on the news as a reporter stood in front of it doing a live report. I could see Jay standing there with his hands on his head. Through all of the chaos, I hadn't even called him. I asked Baker for his phone. He ended the call he was on and handed me his phone. It started ringing before I could make the call.

"Hello," I answered.

"What the fuck happened? I just went to yo' house, and it was burned the fuck down! Where my niece and nephews? They cool? You okay? Where Baker?" Jay shouted.

"I'm okay and the boys are too. Londyn's arm got burned. Baker is with me."

"Damn sis. Is it bad? How the house catch on fire any fuckin' way?" I gave Jay all the information on the kids and my conversation with the police. "Who the fuck set the house on fire? Why would a muthafucka do some shit like that? This some bullshit man!" Jay yelled.

Baker asked me for the phone, I passed it to him. "Aye bruh it's the same person that was feeding Zell information." Baker said when he got on the phone.

"Maaaaaaaan you lyin'. What hospital y'all at? I'm on my way up there." Jay was so loud and upset I could hear what he was saying, and the phone wasn't on speaker.

"South Suburban."

Jay got to the hospital within minutes. Him and Baker were able to have an in-depth conversation about what happened and how Baker came across his information about Kee. Jay went to sit in the room with Londyn then the twins for a little while. He came back with a crazy look on his face.

"They gon' get it. My muthafuckin' niece laying there wit' her hand and arm all wrapped up. Wait until I get a hold of that bitch Kee. My nephews only three months old! They shouldn't even be in here! These fuck bitches and this fuck nigga fucked up!" Jay yelled while he paced the floor.

Neither me nor Baker said a word to Jay while he went off. There was no way that we would be able to calm him down. He loved my kids like they were his, and it hurt him to see them hurt just like it did Baker and I. Besides, we felt the same way he felt. My kids are way too young to be going through this type of stuff.

A day later, the kids were discharged, and we all went to Baker's apartment at The Lex on 21st and Indiana. When Baker got this apartment, Londyn claimed the den as hers. Baker painted it pink for her and got her everything she wanted to go in it. B.J. and Zayden's room was painted blue with two cribs in it and basketball decorations on the walls.

I got them settled in their rooms and went to lay in Baker's bed. He left back out of the door five minutes after we got there. I was a little scared because he left me alone. He assured me that nothing would happen to me or the kids while we were here.

I was really worried about him making it back and if he was really okay about Starks. He seemed to be down at times, but I wasn't gon' ask him about it. He said he didn't wanna talk about it at the hospital, and I was honoring his wish.

I curled up in his bed that he hadn't slept in for days. It still had his scent on it. I inhaled and prayed to God that Baker made it back here today. I hugged his pillow and watched TV until I drifted off in a deep sleep.

Baker

Cola and my lil ones were settled at my house, and I had a run to make. I needed to set some shit for Saudia up. I wasn't wasting no time getting at her. We made that mistake wit' Zell, and I was not doing it again. From now on, we handling shit as soon as we find out what was up. I didn't care who wanted do what. We could have been killed Zell bitch ass, but Co wanted to do shit her way, and it got me shot and her raped wit' a fuckin' stick. I wasn't giving nobody else a chance to do that shit again.

I pulled up to Kira and Goo's house in the 100's and checked the scenery before I got out my car. Everything looked aight to me. I hopped out my Porsche and headed to the door. I planned on being in and out of here in less than twenty minutes. I had to get back to Co. I had somethin' I had do tonight too.

"What up doe?" I said when Goo opened the door.

"What's good? The kids and Cola cool?" He asked when we got to the kitchen.

"Yeah, they all good. I just dropped them off at my crib on Indiana."

"You got them in the honeycomb hideout," Goo laughed. Only a few people knew where I laid my head. I had a house over East that I never slept at. Every night I would go park my car in front of the house, walk in like I'm laying it down, but I would really slip out the back and go to the garage. I would come out in a different car then go to my real crib on 21st and Indiana. In my lifestyle, I had to be careful. I wished I was being like that when Kee followed me to Co's crib. I slacked hard as hell on that. That fire was my fault.

"So, what's up wit' Kee and Saudia? Jake told me bits and pieces of it last night. I need all the details." Goo sat there wit' his mouth open when I told him what was up. He agreed wit' me that Saudia's brother was probably responsible for Starks being gone. "I don't believe my nigga gone, Baker. That shit crazy. Who is her brother anyway?"

"Yeah, it is. I can't believe that shit either. Cuz should be right here going over this shit wit' us. I don't know who her brother is. Saudia pulled one on me. She had me thinking she was the only child."

"Damn. So, what's the plan?"

"Since Saudia never met Jay. He gon' play the role of a sucka. You know how them thirsty niggas be. Jay gon' tell her he was gon' take her shopping and get her hair done the next day. I got everything else lined up already. I need you to get them needles for me." Goo knew exactly what I wanted from him. I couldn't wait to give Saudia her payback.

"Oh, shit. I got you."

I left Goo's crib and went to get Cola some hygiene and hair products. I grabbed her some socks and some of them footies she liked to walk around the house in, too. Since I was shopping, I bought the kids a few things. After I left the first store, I went to the mall. I got Co a couple pairs of Air Max and a few pairs of Jordan's.

Victoria's Secret wasn't ready for me. I had all her favorite scents in one bag and another two bags full of panties and bras for her. From there, I drove to the Levi's store and got her a few pairs of jeans and shorts. They only had a few shirts that she would like. I would have to take her shopping to let her pick out what she wanted at a later date.

Before I headed home, I made sure I wasn't being followed by circling a few blocks during the drive. I called Cola to see if she wanted somethin' to eat. She said she was cooking tonight. Wit' that being said, I jumped on the E-way and went straight home. Jay called me when I was pulling into my parking spot and told me he got Saudia's number and he would hit me later wit' the time he would be picking her up tomorrow for her fake hair appointment.

It was six in the evening, when I walked through the door. Cola had it smelling good in here. I couldn't wait to get a plate of whatever she was cooking. She was standing at the stove in a pair of my boxers and one of my t-shirts. I used to love seeing her wear that around the house.

Having Co around was helping me cope wit' Starks' death. Just the way she looked at me when she knew I was thinking about him calmed me down a lot. My kids kept my spirits up too while I mourned Starks. It was time I get my family back together.

"What you in here burning up?" I asked from the door. I walked further in the house wit' both of my hands and arms full of bags.

"Fried chicken, baked mac and cheese, collard greens, and some nasty sweet potatoes for you and Londyn. I can't stand them things. And it won't be burned thank you very much," she smiled.

"That chicken gon' be crispy, but it's still gon' be bleeding on the inside," I laughed.

"Shut up, Baker," Cola laughed as she opened the oven to check on the macaroni and cheese. "I hope you don't mind me wearing your stuff. I took a shower and didn't have nothing to put on."

"I don't mind you wearing it." Co just didn't know I loved seeing her in my clothes. I wanted grab her and kiss all over her right now. I was gonna save all that for later on tonight.

"You been shopping for the kids or for yourself?" Cola asked as she washed her hands.

"I got them some stuff, but I went for you. The kids got everything they need over here already. You lost everything. I got you a few things to start you off in. I'll take you shopping to get the lil ones some stuff and whatever you need when you ready."

"Thanks, Baker. You didn't have to do that for me. The money you give me every month is more than enough to take care of me and the kids. I have some money put up. I'll pay you back."

"You crazy. I ain't taking no money from you." The smoke detector started beeping, "Aw shit. I told you; you was gon' burn some shit up."

She playfully hit me in the chest and fanned the smoke detector. She checked the food and told me it was ready. She called Londyn out of the back to come eat. Londyn ran to me and gave me a kiss. My lil lady told me she missed me all day. She was smiling and being herself. I was happy to see that. Londyn and Cola sat at the table while me and my boys were chillin' on the couch.

After we ate, Londyn wanted her toes polished. Cola cleaned her arm and put a clean gauze on it before they had some girl time. Me and my boys had a boys' night in. We was chillin' catching up on what was happening in the sports world. I looked down at Cola's toes, and they were a fuckin' mess. Londyn's right arm got burned, which meant she had to do Cola's toes wit' her left hand. She had polish everywhere except Cola's toenails. Co just smiled and told her she was doing a good job.

The kids went to sleep, and Cola was cleaning the kitchen up. I was putting everything I got for her earlier in the closet when my Aunt Carla called me to tell me Starks' funeral would be in a few days. I told her to call me if she needed anything. I didn't wanna go see my cousin in a casket, but I had to pay my respects. That phone call really made me wanna get my family back right.

"You gon' take that polish off yo' toes?" I asked Co when I walked in the kitchen.

"No. My baby did this with one good hand. It's staying on until it comes off," Cola said as she finished washing the last pot.

"I need to talk to you about somethin'." I grabbed her hand and walked her to my bedroom. I shut the door behind her and started talking, "That shit wit' Starks, tell me about that."

"Baker no. We in a good place right now and I want it to stay like this. I don't wanna talk about nothing that will make us argue," she said as she tried to get to the door. We had more than a few disagreements over the last few months over this topic. This time would be different. Even though Starks was gone I needed the unanswered questions I had answered. My curiosity would always get to me when it came to this if we didn't talk about it. Before we got back together, I wanted to know everything.

Lightly grabbing her arm I said, "I promise we not gon' get into it. I'm asking you about it for a reason." Cola explained everything that went on between her and my cousin. She didn't leave nothing out. Some of that shit she told me about I wish she would have left out, but I asked for it.

She cried when she told me she thought I would leave her if I knew and that's the only reason she kept it from me. I believed her the first time she told me that. At the time, I couldn't accept the fact that the woman I loved more than anything kept some shit like that from me.

"Stop crying," I said as I wiped her tears. "No matter how hard I tried I couldn't stop loving you, Co. When I saw you in that car unconscious, I thought I wouldn't get a chance to tell you how I been feeling. I love yo' ass wit' my soul man. I want my family back. Straight up."

"I love you, too, Baker. I never stopped loving you either. It was hard for me to pretend I was cool with you being with other women. I hated that someone other than me was making you happy. I wanna be the only one that makes you happy," Cola said sincerely.

"You the only one that can make me happy, Co. I wasn't happy without you. I thought about you every day. I want you and only you," I leaned in and kissed her soft lips. After all this time, she still had a crazy hold on my heart.

"Do I get my ring back?" Cola asked as she undressed me.

"Damn you trying to lock me down already? We ain't been back together two minutes, and you already want a ring," I laughed. "You got my heart and you got this ring." I pulled out the same ring I gave her on her birthday last year. I didn't ask for it back, partially because deep down I knew she was gon' be wearing it again. Cola forced me to take the ring when she put it in Londyn's bag one day when I picked her up.

Cola put the ring on her finger, pushed me on the bed, and gave me the ride of my life. I missed our sex, her touch, her lips, her smell, and everything else about her. I put it down all night and half of the morning until the kids woke up. I needed that session wit' all the stress I been under. Surprisingly, my boys slept all night. I think they knew what I was on and didn't wanna interrupt. My lil lady used to be a cockblocker when she was a baby. Anytime I got close to Co; she would cry. My boys knew what was up.

I got up and made Londyn somethin' to eat so Cola could get some sleep. I fed and changed my boys after I made Londyn some oatmeal. Londyn took a bath and started playing wit' her toys. It felt good to have my lil ones and Cola all here as a family. I missed this in my life.

Later on that afternoon, Londyn started to complain about her arm hurting. My lil lady telling me her arm hurt put me back in a bad mood. Anybody that knew me know my lil ones were my heart. If a muthafucka harmed them, it was a price to pay. Kee and anybody else that wanna get involved was about to pay that price.

I gave Londyn some pain medication, cleaned her arm, and sat in her room wit' her until she fell asleep. The twins were already taking a nap, and it was time for me to get ready to go see Saudia. I jumped in the shower, put on some dark blue Levi's, a black t-shirt and some black and royal blue Air Max 95's.

I woke Cola up and told her I would be back later on. I let her know the kids were sleep and left her some money to order a pizza or somethin' so she wouldn't have to cook tonight. I gave her a kiss, threw on a royal blue fitted, grabbed my keys, and left.

Before I went to the shop, I had a stop to make. I got in my Range and drove the few blocks to the Dearborns to pick Goo up. Him and Jake were in the parking lot on 27th and State next to Jake's car when I pulled up. I talked to Jake for a minute about some dope I needed him to pick up and drop off for me while I was at the shop. Jay called me and said Saudia was under the dryer, and she would be getting in the chair in about twenty minutes. Goo hopped in my car and showed me what I asked him to get for me.

We drove to some shop out in Roseland. Kira knew the manager and was able to get the keys to the salon. Her and Kimmy were playing the role of hairdressers. It didn't matter if Saudia noticed them. Once she got there, she was stuck. Wasn't no leaving the shop until I let her leave.

Since it was a Sunday, we knew it would look odd that the shop was open. I had Xotica and her friend, Pinky go to the shop before Jay came through wit' Saudia. Kira and Kimmy didn't know shit about doing hair. Xotica and Pinky went in the shop wit' their already done hair wrapped up in scarves.

They sat in the shop and gossiped for a couple hours waiting on Jay to let Kira know when he was five minutes away. When it was time to go, Xotica and Pinky let their hair down and walked right by Saudia and Jay looking like they had actually gotten their hair done.

Goo and me walked in to see Jay sitting in a chair looking like he was bored. Kimmy was sitting in a chair complaining about how her fake client was always late. Saudia had just sat down in the chair she thought she would be getting her hair done in when Goo put a pistol to her head. Kimmy got up to close the blinds and lock the door.

Goo kept the pistol to Saudia's head. She was begging Jay to help her. He looked at her, picked up a magazine, and flipped through the pages. She started to cry when she recognized the faces of people she met a few times before. Her eyes grew wide when she realized what was happening.

Kira walked around to the front of her chair and smacked Saudia wit' some hot flat irons. It left a big ass red mark on her face. Saudia screamed and tried to run. Kimmy pulled out a .38 and stopped her dead in her tracks.

"What I do?" she cried as she held her face.

"You thought I wasn't gon' find out you the reason my daughter got burned. My girl and my kids' lives got put in danger because of you and I wanna know the reason for it."

"Baker, I swear I don't know what you talking about."

"Have a seat Saudia." She backed up into the chair. "I got some questions and you gon' give me some answers. You either gon' answer wit' words or you gon' answer wit yo' life," I said as Kira pulled out a .9 and pointed it in Saudia's direction. Saudia had a look of terror on her face. "Don't lie to me Saudia. Who is Pooh?" I asked as I put my hands in my pocket.

"Me. My mother gave me that nickname when I was little because I loved Winnie the Pooh. When I got older, I started to go by my real name," she said as tears fell from her face.

"So you and Kee sisters, huh?"

"Bitch you better tell every fuckin' thing or else I'mma blast yo' brains all over the wall and send them bitches to yo' mama in a gift box," Jay said as he put a Glock 40 in the chair next to him.

"Yes. Kee is my sister on my mama's side," Saudia said in a shaky voice.

"How you and Kee get in tune wit' each other?" I asked since Kee never told Cola she talked to her sister.

"Me and Kee have been in touch with each other for years. I went to visit somebody in the hospital a few years back. Kee was her nurse. That's how we reconnected." Saudia kept looking around the room trying to find an escape route. She could forget that. She wouldn't make it out the chair before she felt that hot shit.

"Kee was one slick bitch," Jay stated. Kee had all of us thinking she didn't know where her sister was. Come to find out they been in contact wit' each other for a minute.

"I'm sorry. I never meant for your kids to get hurt. That was all Kee," she cried.

"Dry them tears Saudia they ain't gon' help you," I said.

"I'm so sorry, Baker. Please don't kill me. Please," she pleaded.

"Damn that attitude changed a lot. Wasn't you a soft ass nigga not too long ago?" Goo asked being sarcastic about the shit Saudia said about me.

"What a difference a day makes," Jay said still flipping through the magazine.

"You pregnant," I asked as I put on two pairs of latex gloves.

"No. That was my neighbor's test," Saudia cried. Those waterworks wasn't gon' save her. She was part of the reason my kids got harmed, so she gotta get dealt wit'. I was glad she wasn't pregnant. That would change what I had in store for her. I didn't fuck wit' kids' lives. Born or unborn, that was somethin' that didn't sit well wit' me.

"How Kee know where the wedding was gon' be?" I knew the answer to this already since Saudia knew about the wedding. Shit made sense why Kee just popped up after this long on that particular day.

"I told her about it. Baker, I swear I didn't know she was gon' do nothing to yo' baby mama. I just told her Jay was getting married. She asked me when and where, and I told her. I swear on my life I didn't know she was gon' do anything. Baker please forgive me for all of this." Saudia was sitting in the chair begging me not to kill her. She didn't have to beg me. I didn't have no intentions on taking her life. Not today, tomorrow, next week, or next month. The only thing I wanted to do was fuck her life up.

"Let me get that, Goo." He handed me the plastic bag that contained five needles. Three full of heroin and two needles filled wit' a mixture of heroin and coke. "One more thing Saudia. Who is yo' brother?" That was what I really need to know. If I could find out who he was, I could find out what problem he had wit' us and solve it quick for him.

"I don't have a brother, Baker," Saudia lied. I asked her more than once, and she kept lying to me. She was protecting her brother. She was not giving him up at gunpoint. I didn't know who he was, but before it was over, he gon' regret saying my fuckin' name.

Kimmy and Kira tucked their guns and held Saudia down in the chair. Goo held her feet down, while Jay had his Glock pointed at her head. I approached Saudia slowly. I tapped her arm until a vein popped out. Saudia was screaming saying how sorry she was and if we let her go she would go to another country.

Her cries and apologies didn't mean shit to me. I stuck the needle in her vein and injected her wit' her first dose of heroin. Kimmy, Kira, and Goo let go of Saudia and watched the effects the heroin had on her. Her eyes rolled in the back of her head, and she slipped into a nod as the drug took over her.

Saudia thought by telling me about Kee I would spare her the consequences of her actions. She was wrong. She was in on all this shit. Plus this bitch was reporting to some bitch ass nigga about us. She had to pay in some kind of way for what she did. Just because I didn't kill or beat women didn't mean they wouldn't feel me if they crossed me.

After she came down off that high, I found a vein in her other arm. This time I stuck a needle full of heroin and coke mixed together in her arm. I wanted to make sure Saudia was addicted to drugs before she left the shop. Hours were spent in the shop introducing Saudia to her new best friend. I used every needle except for one, only because I didn't want her to overdose. I wanted her to live the rest of her life addicted to heroin.

Right after I was done wit' Sadia, Kira combed her hair into a neat ponytail to make it look like she'd actually gotten her hair done. Jay put a small bag of heroin in Saudia's pocket. In due time, she would figure out what to do wit' it.

"You still don't wanna tell me who yo' brother is Saudia?" I asked before Kira let her get up.

Saudia was still high as a kite, but I heard her when she mumbled the name, "Dan." Kimmy unlocked the door, and Saudia stumbled out of the shop high out of her mind.

"Remind me never to cross you, Baker. Shit. You just fucked that girl's life up," Kimmy said.

"Well, I'll be damned," Kira said as she stared at me wit' a smile on her face.

"You a vicious nigga at times, Baker," Goo shook his head.

"Now that's how you get a muthafucka back without killing them," Jay said.

"We need to find out what Dan look like. Ain't no small time nigga coming at us. Matter of fact, Kira you still talk to Jazzy?"

"Sometimes. She got some fat sloppy ass nigga she mess wit'. She be all under him for that cash now."

"If you get in touch wit' her ask her about him. Everybody else y'all know the routine," I said before I left the shop to go spend some time wit' Co.

None of my people, wit' the exception of Goo and Jake knew what I had planned for Saudia. They all probably thought I was gon' kill her. That would have been too easy of a punishment for her. I wanted her to suffer for her role in this shit. She was gon' lose her house, her car, and her mind trying to get high. I could have easily taken her life quickly. Instead, I decided to kill her slowly. Saudia would regret what she did for the rest of her heroin-addicted life.

Now that I knew her brother's name it was about to be a game of cat and mouse. I had a feeling shit' was gon' get worse before it got better.

Jay

Kee ain't been in or out this hotel in days. I was starting to wonder if she was even staying there. I checked in every hour on the hour wit' the youngin's I had watching the hotel. They were at every angle of the hotel wit' multiple pictures of Kee in their phones. I didn't want nobody to miss her because she didn't look like her picture or some shit. A fuck up on this job wasn't gon' fly wit' me. Kee had to die, and that was the only way I would be happy.

I adjusted the collar of my dress shirt before I put my jacket on. Today was Starks' funeral. I was going to support Baker and his family. Plus Co begged me to go because she didn't think she would feel comfortable being there. Not to be harsh, but he dead and Baker was over what happened between them. I guess I would have to be in her shoes to understand where she was coming from.

I had to leave to go pick Marlene up from work before we went to the funeral. She worked the overnight shift just so she could make it. She didn't know Starks. She was going for the same reason I was going, support.

While driving to the North side, I started thinking about how crazy life was. I took a couple lives before, and mine had been spared more than once. Zell wasn't the only nigga that tried to kill me. He was just the only one that actually came close to doing it. My gut was telling me that I wasn't gon' keep cheating death the way I had been.

"Why are you late?" Marlene asked when she got in the car.

"I'm like three minutes late. Stop trippin'." I was really forty-five minutes late, but I'm here now. She needs to cut a nigga some slack.

"It's raining and I've been standing out here for almost an hour, Jay. What were you doing that had you late to pick me up?"

"Girl you don't see all this sexy in front of you? That's what I was doing."

Marlene laughed, "Be on time tomorrow Jay."

"Yes master."

I pulled off and cut my music up loud. My nigga Kevin Gates was blessing my speakers. I had to cut it right back down when my phone rang. Every time somebody called my phone when I was about to jam out; it was bad news. I looked at my phone and saw it was a number from the joint. I answered the phone and accepted the call after I heard the recorded name that was said.

"Richie Rich what's up wit' it? I said to my longtime friend. "A nigga did what to my pops?...Did he survive?....Who the fuck did it?....Fuck them recording this call! A nigga stabbed my pops! I can't do shit to that fuck nigga in jail!" I barked into the phone.

Out of my peripheral vision, I saw a blue Crown Vic pull up right next to me while I was at a red light wit' my phone to my ear. When the light turned green, I pulled off. The Crown Vic was doing the exact same speed as me. Marlene was steady tapping me on my arm to get my attention. I looked past her and saw a Desert Eagle in my direction....To be continued.

Nicole Black, whose real name is Nicolette, was born and raised on the south side of Chicago. Her love of reading has always gotten her through tough times. During a rough patch, instead of reading she decided to write. After months of writing, Nicole passed her finished book around to close friends who urged her to get it published. Her first book, titled Chi-Town Hood Affairs was published on 9/3/14. Nicole is still a resident of Chicago where she is working and raising her son.

ation can be obtained
ing.com
A
519
7B/958

9 781502 966759